KICKBACK

about the author

Michael Hardcastle was born in Huddersfield in Yorkshire, and after leaving school he served in the Royal Army Educational Corps in England, Kenya and Mauritius. Later he worked for provincial daily newspapers in a variety of writing roles, from reporter and diarist to literary editor and chief feature writer.

He has written more than one hundred children's books since the first one was published in 1966, but he still finds time to visit schools and colleges all over Britain to talk about books and writing. In 1988 he was appointed MBE in recognition of his services to children's books. He is married and lives in Beverley, near Hull.

KICKBACK

Michael Hardcastle

faber and faber

LONDON · BOSTON

First published in 1989
by Faber and Faber Limited
3 Queen Square London WC1N 3AU
This paperback edition first published in 1992
Printed in England by Clays Ltd, St Ives plc

A CIP record for this book is available from
the British Library.
ISBN 0–571–16505–2

One

There was just enough light in the morning sky for Ros to see her way across to the yard. Already she could hear the sounds of the restless ones, the horses that hardly ever stopped moving; the horses that wanted breakfast now, not an hour later; the horses that were suffering some discomfort or simply couldn't get used to their new surroundings. But the only one she was thinking about was Mantola. She was listening for him when she stepped on the rake that flew up and cracked her very painfully on the knee.

She swore. It was the sort of word her friends and fellow workers in the stable had never heard her utter. And she wouldn't have used it at all if any of them had been within earshot. In a racing stable, strong language is part of everyday life and most people don't even know they are using it. Tildown House wasn't a racing stable but Angela Sagaro ran it like one. In any case, most of the occupants of the boxes had spent at least part of their careers on the racetracks of England or Ireland or even France.

'That's another black mark on your scoresheet, Lydia Kent,' muttered Ros, knowing with total certainty who was responsible for leaving a rake where it could be trodden on. She massaged her knee through her jodhpurs and imagined the size of the bruise that would be the legacy. She added wryly: 'Well, it makes a change from bothering about *your* knees, Mantola. Or the rest of your legs, come to that.'

She remembered to pick up the rake and place it with the rest of the equipment just inside the tack room. Mantola was only two boxes away now and she could hear his snorting: louder, quicker, more urgent than any other horse's. He didn't whinny or make any of the other customary horse noises. It was just another thing that set him apart from the rest, from the common herd, as she sometimes expressed it (though never in Mrs Sagaro's hearing).

A few strides from his box she paused to listen: listen intently. By now she believed she could tell just by the sound of his movements how he was feeling and what sort of night he'd spent. Nowadays he seemed to know what *she* was doing, too, and that he ought to reassure her by slowing down. But this morning he was moving more briskly than ever, turning, turning, turning, tail swishing, breath snorting out.

'Oh dear,' she said, her voice now well above a whisper, 'you've had another poor night, haven't you? So your bed will be in a terrible state and you'll look grumpy and not at all as lovely as you should be. Oh dear. Oh, Manty, what *are* we going to do with you?'

As she talked she was unwrapping the boiled sweet in her pocket. Every day, without fail, Mantola received his present for surviving the night and wanting to see her. He accepted it rather cautiously and always with dignity: there was no agitated snuffling or boisterous behaviour of the kind she'd expect in another horse. Mantola took his reward with the style of a monarch. Ros told him so even if she didn't dare tell anyone else for fear of being laughed at. She was well aware that some people, like Lydia, thought she was too fond of the horse in her charge. Too fond for her own good, they said. Because one day the horse would leave Tildown House to return to his owner or trainer.

Swiftly now she slipped back the bolts on the half-doors and, saying 'Hey there, Manty, hey, hey, hey', stepped into the box. In the gloom he wasn't easy to see at first. She didn't put the light on because she knew he hated that; on the first occasion she'd done so he'd reared so high he seemed to be in danger of cracking his skull on the ceiling. After that it had taken him hours to settle down and respond to her gentle ways. Mantola was as dark a bay as you could find but no one in the racing world would describe him as black because black was thought to be unlucky. So, officially, he was a brown horse.

Now he edged forward, nostrils flickering in anticipation of the pleasures of that boiled sweet and the comforting touch of Ros's hands on his neck and flanks. He took the sweet from her palm and happily began to crunch away as she stroked him.

'Good, Manty, good, Manty,' she murmured as, carefully, she slid her hands down his legs, searching for the tendons that had caused him so much pain, so many problems.

'Oh, thank goodness!' she exclaimed. For she could feel none of the 'burny' heat she'd more than half expected to find. The inflammation had receded in spite of his energetic walking. He was getting better! She wanted to reward him with another sweet but that had to be resisted; it would become a habit, a 'soft habit that can weaken a horse's natural attitudes to life', as Angela Sagaro expressed it. Horses, declared the stable's owner, must never be treated like domestic pets. They were noble, self-contained individuals with dignity and pride, not fat, wimp-like lapdogs who'd perform any trick for a tasty soft centre. Ros completely agreed with her.

In any case, Mantola had, as usual, annoyingly got rid of the bandage on his off-fore by gripping it with his teeth and somehow shaking it free. So Ros's first task was to replace it, coating it first with the vile-smelling concoction containing fuller's earth and vinegar and the secret ingredient that their vet swore by but would never give a name to.

3

'And just look at your bed!' Ros declared indignantly. 'Oh Manty, surely you don't have to make *such* a mess!'

The straw bedding looked as though it had been fed through a shredding machine. The horse's perpetual nocturnal pacing, pursuing a triangular pathway for hours on end, had devastated the floor covering. It would take Ros ages to clear it up instead of just having to fork out the dirty straw and the droppings. When Mantola had been in that mood, mucking out was a marathon task.

She reached up to fondle one of his ears, something he'd allow no one else to do at any time. A stalls handler on a racecourse who'd once tried to tug at his ears to calm him down had been bitten quite severely, Mrs Sagaro had told Ros. That was really the beginning of the end for Mantola as a racehorse. He was getting the reputation of being a rogue and a danger to himself and any human being who came in range when he was in one of his moods. But he'd never shown any resentment when Ros's fingers explored the softness of those restless ears.

'Do you know what Lydia thinks?' she asked him, and he turned to look at her as if about to participate in a conversation. 'She thinks you ought to have somebody, well, some *companion*, I suppose, to keep you company in your box at night. Not entirely daft, our Lydia, you know. She reckons that would cure you of stalking round and round all night like somebody on sentry duty. What d'you think, Manty?'

As she manoeuvred him around the box during the tidying-up operation she kept talking, knowing that he liked the sound of her voice. She'd once read what she thought was a significant comment: 'The more you humanize a horse, the more human he becomes.' Well, she knew a lot of people didn't agree with that attitude, or even believe it could possibly be true. A horse was an animal like any other four-legged creature and should be treated like the rest: that is, as completely inferior in every way to a human being. Ros could never support an attitude like that.

She was convinced that horses were perfectly capable of picking up feelings in the air and responding to them. Kindness was her style and Mantola liked it that way, she was convinced. In any case, like nearly all the other horses at Tildown House, he was there for the good of his health, physical health or mental health or, in some cases, both at the same time. Tildown House was an equine nursing home or, more properly, a convalescent home, and Mantola was one of the patients. If he didn't improve, then not only were his racing days over, his life would be at risk. If all treatment failed, Mantola might soon finish up as dog meat. Ros shuddered.

'So, what do you think, Manty?' she asked as she scraped away the last of the mess on the floor and dumped the discarded bandage. 'Lydia has the funny notion that you ought to have a goat for company. How d'you fancy that, eh?'

Mantola's big brown eyes followed her as she moved around the box with scraper and bucket, brush and sponge. He always seemed to know if she was asking him a serious question and then he was completely calm. Ros couldn't really imagine him tolerating another animal in his private box but Lydia insisted that lots of horses adored goats and that, once a friendship was established, the two were inseparable. Lydia had plenty of faults – carelessness in leaving tack and equipment about, arriving late for work, being forgetful when memory was important – but there was no denying that she knew a lot about horses and their sometimes odd behaviour. More important than anything, she cared about them just as deeply as Ros did. For that, Ros could forgive her almost anything. Lydia's father was a former jockey, now working very successfully as private chauffeur to a millionaire racehorse owner, and it was from him that Lydia had learned so much equine lore.

Suddenly, Mantola's ears shot forward as he picked up the sound of someone else in the yard. He moved towards the door but Ros leaned her shoulder into his chest and pushed him back.

'Not yet, not yet,' she told him. 'I know Lydia's arrived but you won't be getting your grub yet. It's exercise-time first, remember. And I'm going to take you on a lovely gallop today. You'll love every minute of it. You *know* you will. Your legs are fine so there's nothing for you to worry about. Or me, really.'

In fact, Mantola hadn't done any serious work for some weeks. So there was no way of knowing how his rather fragile tendons would stand up to the strain of his being ridden at speed. Mrs Sagaro had given her opinion on the matter the previous day: she thought Mantola was sound as a bell again and ought to be tackling some real work, if only to see how he reacted to it.

But, she added, there was no point in employing good staff if she didn't trust them. So that was why the decision as to how hard Mantola worked was left to the girl who looked after him: Ros Hayward. That was a responsibility Ros herself viewed with some trepidation. After all, a real racehorse like Mantola was worth a lot of money and so she wasn't anxious to make any decision that might lead to a devaluation of the horse. The owner wouldn't want to hear that his horse had suffered yet another setback and accordingly would require a prolonged period of rest. Horses cost a lot of money to keep in a place like Tildown House. Owners, to listen to Angela Sagaro, were always going on about the exorbitant charges for pills and injections and bandages provided by the vet, for new 'plates' (shoes, to non-racing types) from the farrier and, naturally, for the food and accommodation and kindness that kept their horses alive. 'Sometimes,' said Mrs Sagaro dolefully, 'I wonder why they bother to have a horse in the first place when they begrudge every penny they spend on it. Still, if they *didn't* own the horse *we* wouldn't be in business, would we?'

'So, you see, we've got to be very careful, Manty,' Ros, remembering all that, told him as she completed the clearing up. 'If you'll be patient for another three minutes I'll saddle you up and away we'll go.'

But then, before she could take another step, the top half of the door swung open and Lydia was grinning in at them. Mantola's nose wrinkled at the prospect of another titbit. Lydia's generosity, however, was unpredictable and she had nothing for him this morning.

'Hey,' she said eagerly, 'want to hear the news?'

'Is it good or bad?'

'Depends on how you're feeling today,' Lydia answered with a laugh. Because her own manner was invariably cheerful it was often impossible to tell what her feelings were about anything. Lydia could be quite unrealistic about life.

'Well, I know one thing I'm feeling, Lydia,' Ros told her. 'I'm mad at you. You very nearly crippled me this morning.'

Lydia's eyes opened wider than usual. When she ran her fingers through her mass of brown curls like that she was marvellous at conveying amazement. 'What on earth happened?' she asked with a gasp that was perfectly genuine.

'I stepped on a rake that shot up and cracked me on the knee, that's what happened. It was horribly painful, still is. A rake, Lydia, that *you* must have left lying in the middle of the yard. Trust me to find the perfect bit to step on so that it whacked me on the kneecap!'

'Oh, sorry, Ros! Honestly, I never thought – I mean, I didn't know I'd left anything lying about. Are you, well, *really* hurt?'

Her concern was genuine, as Ros had known it would be: Lydia would walk an extra mile rather than tread on a beetle, though she could be quite tough with any animal that was proving mulish or wouldn't co-operate.

'I'll survive – I think. But in future *please* make sure you put everything away before you leave. You never know, it

7

might be Angela who steps on the next rake and then your days will be numbered.'

'Don't I know it!' Lydia said fervently, reaching out to tickle Mantola's inquisitive nose. 'I think she'll invent an excuse to get rid of me if she can't find one. Honestly, Ros, you know I'd never let her down if – '

'I know, I know,' Ros cut in, not wanting to hear the same old story of how Lydia did her level best at all times but Mrs Sagaro wouldn't make allowances for even the teeniest error of judgment or forgive an instant of forgetfulness. 'Look, what's this news, then? I'm just about ready to take Manty up on Bowler Hill. You know, I think he's really – *really* – sound at last.'

'Well, this bit of information will remove the joy from your soul. Tony Vasson is coming down to ride some work. Should be here any minute now.'

'Oh no!' Ros wailed.

Tony Vasson was Angela Sagaro's brother although they were so unlike that Lydia maintained that Tony had to be an adopted sibling. He and his sister didn't really get on but, the girls suspected, he had some sort of hold over her. A freelance jockey with retainers for a couple of very small stables, he lived in a neighbouring village and only occasionally visited Tildown House. But when he did it was usually to ride work on a horse that was practically ready to be returned to its own stable as fit to resume its racing career. It was an opportunity for him to assess its capabilities and, if he thought highly of them, tout for a ride from the horse's trainer or owner.

As much as anything, it was Tony Vasson's manner that the girls detested. For he tended to treat them like servants of the lowest possible order, regarding them as being provided for his personal benefit. His arrogance was dreadful, Lydia tended to whisper to anyone who would listen to her opinions. For he wasn't one of the country's leading jockeys. Far from it. He rarely had more than a dozen winners in a season. But he gave the impression that he was at least challenging for the Jockeys' Championship each year.

'And do you know what?' Lydia was going on. 'He had the nerve to *telephone* me this morning to say he was coming down here. I mean, phoning *me*! If he's got to announce his intentions, why didn't he phone up his darling sister?'

'Oh well, that's obvious! He wouldn't want to disturb her beauty sleep, would he? He wouldn't be so much in favour if he woke her before she was ready to get up.'

'True, but that's not the only reason, I reckon. He just doesn't want her to know how hard he rides some of our horses. You know he's not supposed to try them out to the limit but he jolly well does when he's in the mood.'

'And Angela wouldn't believe us if we told her,' Ros remarked and Lydia nodded. 'I just wish she could see what he gets up to. When did he say he'd be here?'

Lydia glanced at her wristwatch. 'Right now!' she exclaimed. 'He said twenty minutes and that was precisely twenty minutes ago. But maybe that was just to gee us up to be ready for when he does condescend to arrive. Could be he won't be here for *another* twenty minutes. Be just like him to get us to sweat for nothing.'

'So we've got a chance to outflank him, then,' Ros responded inspirationally. 'If we go like mad and get our horses out in no time we could be halfway up Bowler Hill before he even arrives. Then he'll have a problem of what to do, whether to give chase in his rotten old car or saddle up his own horse from the ones left behind. OK?'

Lydia frowned. 'He'll go bonkers!'

Ros laughed. 'Well, we won't be here to see it, will we? Come on, Lyd, it's worth a try.'

'I'm with you!' Lydia said excitedly, using one of her favourite expressions. 'I'll beat you to the starting stalls, so I will!'

To Ros's relief, it didn't seem to bother Mantola that he

9

was being rushed into action. Normally she lingered over the entire process of preparing him for an outing, whether it was a canter on the gallops or just a stroll along the lanes around the village. It was really the only time of the day they could guarantee they would have to themselves (except, of course, when Lydia swooped in on them) and so Ros made the most of it. Now everything was happening so fast that Mantola ought to have shown some resentment; but he didn't. He seemed as eager as she was to venture out. Even so, she checked carefully that the bit wasn't awkward for him and that the girths were properly tightened.

Before she led him out of his box she remembered to say hello to Magic Lantern, the rather flashy chestnut in the next box who was also her responsibility. He could be a moody old character sometimes but this morning he was as calm as a sundial. So he was rewarded with the spare sweet, and he plainly appreciated it.

'See you soon, Magic,' she promised as she walked Mantola out of the yard.

She was just swinging herself into the saddle when Lydia, already mounted on a very distinctive grey, No Ticket, charged past her.

'Told you I'd be first,' she called delightedly, aiming her horse for the narrow gap into the lane that ran behind the stables. It had become a tradition with them never to use the main gate for their early-morning rides.

'Come on, Pie,' she urged her mount, using the affection-ate name that derived from 'piebald', in honour of the huge darker grey spots on his flanks. And Pie responded as if he, too, was glad to be out of the yard ahead of the visiting jockey.

Mantola seemed equally eager to tackle the sharp ascent of the lower slopes of Bowler Hill. He'd never been asked to race up there in earnest and Ros was looking forward to the day when she could urge him to go at his fastest on the historic training gallops. But that wouldn't be today.

10

Two

The great sweep of the Downs always filled Ros with a sense of awe as well as of joy. To ride up here on a spring morning with the sun coming up and an inviting day ahead of her was an experience guaranteed to bring pleasure. It didn't matter how quietly, or how excitingly, the horse ran: it was enough that they were up there, in a world almost of their own, with a limitless sky on the horizon and no orders to obey. For Angela Sagaro always trusted her girls to do only what was best for the horses in their charge. She knew that they would treat them with love and care, and would employ no one who was unable to establish that level of relationship with them. So whenever Ros took Mantola or Magic Lantern or any other horse to the top of Bowler Hill, she made her own decisions about the severity of the exercise on the gallops. Usually, though, they were there just for the gentlest kind of reintroduction to the world of racing. The real tests would take place when the horse had returned to its home gallops.

'You know, I think we've done it! We've outwitted him!' Lydia called across to her as Ros ranged alongside No Ticket.

Instinctively, Ros glanced behind her – and saw that for once Lydia was quite wrong.

'You spoke too soon, Lyd,' she told her.

'Hell!' Lydia exploded succinctly after a quick look over her shoulder. 'How did he get here so fast? He must have saddled Alex in record time. I didn't think he was capable of even getting into the saddle on his own. Always insists on a leg-up.'

Tony Vasson was riding Alexander's Star, probably the most distinguished racehorse ever to be a temporary inmate of Tildown House Stables. But Alex had developed quite a number of psychological problems, such as refusing to enter starting stalls and lashing out with lethal hooves at any horse he took a sudden dislike to, and so his great speed on the racetrack was no longer of value.

Until he reformed, Alexander's Star wasn't to be allowed near a racecourse again. Hence the trainer's decision to send him to Tildown in the hope that he could be cured of uncivilized behaviour. Because Ros and Lydia were only cantering it was a matter of seconds before Tony Vasson caught up with them.

'I thought I told you to wait for me,' he snapped at Lydia, pulling his mount up with a fierce tug that almost wrenched Alex's head off.

Without being told to, Mantola and No Ticket stopped, too, as if they feared the same harsh treatment was going to be meted out to them.

'Don't *have* to take orders from you,' Lydia responded in a sullen tone, displaying more hostility towards the jockey than Ros had ever seen before. Until that moment she had not realized quite how much Lydia detested the man.

'Reckon you do, if *I* say so,' Tony replied. 'Because if *I* say so then Mrs Sagaro says so. And she just happens to be your boss. The lady who pays your wages. But won't be paying you a single penny if *I* say so.' He paused and then added: 'Because you'll be *fired*, Miss Kent.'

Ros was looking at him as he said all that and she could see the gleam in his close-together eyes, a gleam of pleasure. Tony Vasson was the sort of man who liked to inflict pain and see its effect on his victim. Lydia couldn't bring herself to the point of making any reply at all. Ros wondered if her friend would think it worthwhile to apologize, just to damp down Tony's anger. But Lydia said nothing.

Now Tony glanced across at Ros, as if hoping she'd make some comment; but Ros returned his look as levelly as possible. She didn't want to get into a slanging match with the jockey and she saw no reason to intervene in any way.

'I think I'll have a change today,' Tony announced unexpectedly. He continued to give Ros one of his hard, almost challenging looks. 'I'll ride your horse, Miss Hayward.'

It was part of his act always to address the girls in this arch, pseudo-formal style. It was as if he wanted to impress on them that he was their superior, that he could never be on familiar terms with them. Their response was never to address him by any name at all.

Ros swallowed. This was what she'd feared most. 'He's not ready yet for real work,' she pointed out. 'He's still, well, convalescing. Mrs Sagaro must have told you that. I mean, Mantola needs very careful handling. He's still bandaged, as you can see.'

'They're all convalescing,' Tony replied. 'That's what they're here for.'

'Yes, but some are, well, sort of – special,' Ros floundered, desperately trying to think of a way of protecting Mantola.

'They're all special, too. If we don't try 'em out we'll never find out if they're over the worst,' he said in a perfectly reasonable tone. 'Your fella looks in pretty good shape to me. So let's get aboard, see what he's capable of.'

'But what about Alexander's Star?' Ros asked, still believing that Tony wouldn't abandon the most famous horse in the stable, the horse which had lived up to its name on more than one racetrack in Britain and France. Tony himself had declared several times that it was his intention to turn Alex into a winner again one day.

The jockey was already sliding out of the saddle. As soon as he was standing on the ground he held out the reins to

13

Ros and said with a lopsided grin: 'You can have him. You're always telling us what a brilliant jockey you are. So let's see how you get on with a real racehorse.'

'I've never said that!' Ros protested heatedly. But protests were useless. Tony Vasson had made up his mind what *he* wanted and that was that.

'That's not fair!' Lydia pointed out. 'You shouldn't – '

'Life's not fair,' Tony told her imperturbably. 'If it was, you'd be working in kennels with poodles or greyhounds or some breed like that. They're about your size, your level, Miss Kent.'

'That's a rotten – ' Ros was starting to say when he cut her off with a gesture.

'Come on, Miss Hayward, I'm not waiting all day for you. Get off that horse and get on this one.'

For a moment Ros thought of defying him. *He* wasn't her employer; she wasn't an employee of anyone, not in the proper sense of the word. She worked part-time at Tildown House because she loved being with horses: especially Mantola. The rest of the time she was still at school. But she couldn't bear the thought of being excluded from the stables. And she sensed that that was what might happen if Tony Vasson complained to his sister that Ros Hayward had refused to co-operate with his attempts to exercise the horses and improve their condition. Because that was just what he would do, Ros had no doubt. So she had just about everything to lose and nothing (apart from emotional satisfaction) to gain from not surrendering Mantola to him.

She dismounted.

This time Tony didn't demand a leg-up; very nimbly he vaulted into the saddle. Then he did precisely what Ros had hoped he wouldn't do. 'Look after my fella then,' he said to Ros. 'Don't let him run away with you whatever you do.' And then he gave Mantola a thwack with his whip before urging him forward. Mantola shot away up the slope.

For the second time that morning Ros used a very strong

word to express her feelings. 'Just what I think about him, too,' Lydia agreed fervently.

No Ticket was now moving agitatedly, anxious to continue the canter and follow his stable companion. But Lydia was waiting for Ros to get acquainted with Alexander's Star who was also keen to be on the move. A handsome bay, almost as dark in colouring as Mantola, he had the most powerful quarters Ros had ever seen and a lot of depth in the chest. He was a real speed merchant and Ros couldn't help wondering just how much of that pace he'd retained during his time at Tildown House. In the next few moments she'd probably find out.

'Come on, Ros, we can catch up, make sure he takes good care of Manty,' Lydia urged.

'Well . . .' said Ros doubtfully, thinking that Alexander's Star ought not to be put to the test yet. In the back of her mind, too, was the thought that the big bay just might be tempted to go flat out and see whether he could get the better of her. Being run away with was the fear of every jockey, man or woman; apart from the danger involved, it could be a humiliating experience.

'Oh, come on, Ros! Don't get depressed. You were in a great mood when I saw you in Manty's box.'

The Star had a devouring stride, even up a slope as steep as this one. Within moments he was lengths ahead of his companion: and normally No Ticket quite relished his work on the gallops, always ready to give other horses a lead and show what he was capable of. Now, though, the grey was struggling to draw level in spite of Lydia's encouragement. Neither rider would ever use a whip in a race, let alone on the gallops. At Tildown House the horses were to be treated with kindness and consideration all the time, which was another reason why Ros hated to see Tony Vasson on one of their horses. All he was concerned with was their future prospects on the track, so he wanted to know if they reacted favourably under the most obvious 'stimulus': the whip.

15

For there were plenty of thoroughbreds which so resented the stinging experience that they immediately switched off and became mulish. 'Quitters', the jockeys called them.

Gradually Alex began to respond to Ros's riding and slowed to a fast canter so that No Ticket was able to catch him up. By now, though, Mantola was out of view, somewhere in the depression just below the summit. He must, Ros knew, have been running like the wind. In a way, she hoped he was enjoying himself; part of her, though, believed that Manty could only enjoy himself when she was with him.

'I suppose he could ruin things for you, couldn't he?' Lydia remarked unexpectedly. Her moods changed like a weathervane on a stormy day.

'What?' Ros was taken aback. Minutes earlier Lydia had been expressing optimism. 'Well, his sister will never forgive him if he has hurt Mantola. She'll – '

'I'm not thinking about Mantola's racing career, supposing he's still got one,' Lydia explained. 'I'm thinking about your chances of winning the Midthorpe Marathon on him. I mean, you've set your heart on that, Ros, haven't you?'

Ros had been trying to avoid thinking about the Marathon, though it was always likely to surface in her mind at odd moments of the day. It was the prize she most wanted to win in life and she believed that if Mantola recovered his health in time then they would have a wonderful chance of winning one of the most historic events in the equine calendar. The Midthorpe was unique. For one thing, the allocation of prize money ensured that it was usually more profitable to finish second than to be the winner! But the prestige to be earned by winning this annual cross-country event over a distance of more than four miles was what mattered most to the majority of the competitors. Clearly it also mattered to Sir Alan Needwood, Mantola's owner. He lived in the Midthorpe area and thus was entitled to enter a runner in the Marathon without the horse having to fulfil other conditions first. After the setbacks she'd experienced as a rider in a couple of recent point-to-points Ros needed a boost to her self-esteem. And, as Lydia had supposed, she really had set her heart on winning the Midthorpe.

'I don't suppose Tony will really give Manty a hard time,' she said; but she said it in an uncertain tone.

'Well, he's out of sight now,' Lydia pointed out. 'If we don't get going he'll lose us. Maybe that's what he's got in mind.'

The hill rose some two hundred feet in little more than six furlongs before forming that shallow dip just below the summit. Mantola now reappeared on the rim of this saucer of spongy turf. Plainly Tony was heading for the long ridge that ran away to the left of the summit. Along there he might well demand that Mantola should demonstrate just how fit he was.

Just before you reached the ridge there was a row of rather stunted trees (victims, naturally, of every fierce wind that blew across the Downs). Ros always felt that Manty accelerated when he passed them. But that, she'd been assured by a professional jockey, was really an illusion. Horses always appeared to travel faster when passing trees. Now, glancing towards them, she was astonished to see a man in a green trilby hat using a pair of binoculars. He was standing on something – but what that was she couldn't immediately tell. All she knew was that he was perched at a higher elevation than the land around him; an untidy hedge and dense vegetation prevented her seeing his feet. Surely he hadn't brought a pair of steps with him?

'Who's that then?' she called across to Lydia in a kind of stage whisper.

Lydia looked just as startled as her companion. 'Not a tout, is he? I mean, what would he expect to find up here?'

Touts were usually active only in the vicinity of training areas, hoping to pick up snippets of news about the fitness and performance on the training gallops of a variety of racehorses. Of course, their interpretation of what they witnessed was highly subjective.

Touts had no idea, for instance, what weights the horses might be carrying when they galloped alongside one another or attempted to overtake those in front of them; and they had no real knowledge (only impressions) of what the riders themselves were trying to do with their mounts. All the same, some touts seemed to have a real instinct for analysing what occurred on the training gallops, and their opinions, swiftly communicated to gamblers or book-makers or daily newspapers, could make quite a substantial difference to the odds at which various horses started in subsequent races.

'Must admit, he *looks* like a dubious character!' Lydia added as she and Ros swept past his vantage point.

Quite plainly, their arrival on the scene surprised him. He was staring intently in the direction Mantola had taken. Probably he hadn't expected that anyone else was going to use the gallops at that time because of the interval between Tony's arrival on the scene and then their own. He looked distinctly flustered. But it didn't stop him from continuing his observations.

'Hey, do you know what he's doing?' Lydia asked excitedly after risking a long hard look over her shoulder. 'He's writing things in a notebook. So he *must* be a tout.'

Ros would have glanced round, too, except for the fact that Alex was giving every sign of wanting to stretch out: and stretch out at top speed.

'And do you know what? He's actually standing on the roof of a car! How about that for style,' Lydia called out after another look.

By now Ros was in no position to think about anything except Alex's desire for speed. His sudden acceleration was almost breathtaking. It was as if his rider had pressed a hidden button that sent him instantaneously into over-

18

drive. Ros didn't know whether she was doing the right thing in letting him race away like this.

After all, he was on the 'easy' list at the stables; he was there for the good of his health, not just to show off his paces when he felt like it. But she was practically powerless to check him. Alex wasn't exactly running away with her but, at least for the moment, he was certainly in charge of his own destiny. It was as if he was a star in his own right and had to prove it –

It was also in her mind that Alexander's Star's every flashing stride was bringing them closer to Mantola and Tony Vasson. At the pace they were travelling it really wouldn't be long before they caught them up. Behind them, Lydia was desperately urging No Ticket to close up; but the piebald wasn't capable, even at his very best, of matching strides with a horse as powerful as Alexander's Star. What's more, No Ticket would only exert himself fully when he felt like it, and this morning wasn't one of those times.

In those first few moments when Alex went into over-drive, Ros was actually frightened. In spite of all her experience in the saddle and all the frantic incidents that had happened to her on horseback, she wasn't immune to fright; no one was, if they told the truth. But it was only fleeting, that sudden fear she felt; after a few more raking strides by the big horse, she even began to enjoy the sensation of travelling so fast. It became exhilarating. Up there on the ridge on the edge of the Downs she felt she was almost literally on top of the world. The sky was colossal, the horizon limitless. And Alexander's Star carried her relentlessly nearer to Mantola.

The three runners were well strung out when the man in the green trilby, having seen what he thought he wanted to see, clambered down from the roof of his dark blue saloon and got behind the driving wheel. He'd used an ancient sunken road across the Downs to reach his vantage point:

and one of the advantages of that for him was that the car couldn't easily be seen by those on horseback.

Long before the horses slowed down and then began to turn back, the tout (as Lydia had described him) was heading for home at a rattling pace. He knew that one of the girl riders had spotted him but that didn't matter, he believed. He was confident that the jockey on the big black horse, Tony Vasson, hadn't been aware of his presence. And even if he had, the tout guessed that that wouldn't matter, either.

Tony had turned Mantola at a point midway along the ridge, just before Ros reached them. The jockey eyed his intended mount fairly speculatively.

'This fella seems in pretty good nick,' he told her, slapping Mantola down the shoulder in quite an affectionate way. 'Reckon you've been hiding his light under a bushel.'

To her own surprise, Ros had had no difficulty in pulling Alexander's Star up. The horse apparently realized that he'd done his stuff and could now relax. He was even slowing down before he reached his stable companion. By now Ros wasn't much concerned with Alex – all her anxieties were focused on Mantola, who was blowing hard enough to extinguish a forest fire. Above all she wanted to get down and examine the horse's legs to see whether they'd been affected by his strenuous exertions. But that might look to Tony like a calculated insult. There was no point in antagonizing him unnecessarily. In any case, Mantola would shortly be back in his own box and Ros could attend to him then.

'How d'you get on with this one?' he asked her, nodding at Star. It was fairly obvious he'd expected her to have a problem controlling him.

'Oh, he was fine,' she answered nonchalantly. 'Gave me a terrific ride.'

Tony didn't look as though he quite believed that. 'Sure he didn't run away with you?' he persisted.

'Course not. Wouldn't be here now, would I, if he had?'

This time the jockey wiggled his jaw from side to side as if he were having trouble with the hinges. Ros recognized this as a sign that he wasn't pleased; probably even he would be surprised to know how often he practised that mannerism.

'I expect you want to ride him now, don't you?' Ros added. 'I'll get off so we can swop and – '

'No, I'll take this one back. Let him get used to me. You never know how soon I'll be riding him for real. In a decent race.'

Now Ros didn't know what to say. In a way, Tony was paying her a compliment because it was her devoted care that had restored Mantola to racing fitness (if, that is, he was ready to race). But she still feared that Vasson would ask too much of the horse and thus ruin him for good. But she had no authority, of course, to persuade him to dismount from the horse she looked after and regarded as her own. And Tony wasn't the sort of man who would respond to a polite request.

'See you then,' he announced; and, with one smart slap of the whip on Mantola's flank, they hurtled away towards the stables. The horse was certainly happy to go: he had breakfast on his mind.

'Well, he certainly seems to fancy your old nag, Ros,' Lydia remarked sympathetically, when, somewhat belatedly, she appeared on the scene. No Ticket had earlier decided he'd done enough for one outing and it had taken all of Lydia's persuasive powers to get him to continue along the ridge. Now he was just as eager as Mantola to return home but Lydia believed no horse should get what it wanted immediately it wanted it. One of the reasons Mrs Sagaro employed her was that Lydia was a real disciplinarian when she applied her mind to the task.

'I'm going after them,' Ros said with the same suddenness that Tony had displayed. 'Two can play this game.'

She wasn't being fair and she wasn't being sensible and

21

she knew that. But it didn't prevent her from galvanizing Alexander's Star into action, much to Lydia's surprise. The big horse was just as pleased as Mantola to be heading home and he shot away with his consuming stride. Once again Ros savoured the excitement of riding at speed on a horse that, as one jockey she knew expressed it, 'could catch pigeons without getting up a sweat'. For a moment or two she wondered whether to try to catch up with Mantola; but then she dismissed that idea as foolish and reckless. After all, if she overtook Tony Vasson he'd be thoroughly displeased and probably report her to his sister for taking unwarranted risks with one of her horses. Worse, a chase might develop and then Mantola would suffer from being asked to do too much.

Just once she glanced round and saw that Lydia was following at a sedate pace. No Ticket was in no mood to exert himself even if he was returning to his box and some food. Ros felt rather guilty about almost abandoning Lydia just so that she could keep Mantola in her sights. More than one of her friends had remarked that Ros cared more for Mantola than for any human being; and she supposed that was true. After all, her family didn't seem to be the caring kind. Her parents had split up when Ros was quite small and she hadn't any brothers or sisters. She lived with her mother but in reality all that meant was that they often dwelt under the same roof. Much of the time her mother was away in London, working as a freelance tax consultant. It was a job as mysterious to Ros as the flight deck of an airliner: she had no idea what it involved because it sounded so fantastically complicated. Her mother never attempted to explain any of it to her daughter, for which Ros was really quite greatful. They simply got on with their own lives, their paths merely crossing from time to time.

Most of the staff at her school, as well as her friends, weren't aware of what her home circumstances were really like and fortunately they didn't ask many pertinent questions. But they all knew what Ros felt about working with Mrs Sagaro's horses, especially Mantola.

They were approaching the top of Up-and Down Lane. Alexander's Star, in spite of his keenness to get home, hadn't managed to catch up with Mantola. Ros sensed that her horse, as she always thought of him, had been asked to do too much. He was still convalescent and yet Tony Vasson must have really tried him out. 'Come on, Alex, come on!' she urged the handsome bay; and he responded.

At the bottom of the lane was the pond, the feature of the village that attracted tourists during the summer and when coloured lights were strung across it as part of the Christmas decorations. Ros had totally forgotten that Alexander's Star had a fondness for splashing in that muddy, duck-haunted water whenever he had the chance. Now the big bay turned instinctively towards the pond just as Mantola and Tony Vasson disappeared through the main gates of Tildown House on the opposite side of the lane.

'No, no, this way!' Ros yelled at him, trying to yank his head round so that he would do as she wanted.

Star had always liked his own way in everything – that was one of the problems his trainers found hard to cope with – and he wasn't inclined to take orders from anyone who used force on him. So now, frustrating Ros's orders, he plunged directly across the lane before executing a wicked swerve just as he reached the waterline. Star knew exactly what he was doing and what the outcome of the manoeuvre would be.

Ros hadn't a hope of staying in the saddle. She was catapulted out sideways and head first into the pond. Star, free of restraints, now contentedly entered the water at his own quite sober pace and began to splash about.

Three

Gasping with the shock and the indignity of it all, Ros got to her feet, spraying water in all directions from arms and legs. Although she'd banged her knee painfully (and not the one hurt by the rake, either) on a submerged log, she wasn't really hurt. Her immediate thought was to catch Alexander's Star. Losing control of a valuable racehorse was almost the worst crime she could commit in a trainer's eyes. If Star decided to gallop off on his own, anything could happen to him. For that she would never be forgiven.

Inevitably, the horse was determined not to be caught. His trailing reins were a hidden menace every time he moved; if he entangled himself in those he could easily stumble and, in falling, break a leg.

'Come on, boy, come on!' she pleaded, wading through the water as if it wasn't there. Another soaking was a small price to pay for retrieving the horse without further trouble. But Star, rediscovering the joys of the water, was in a playful mood; so he kept out of her reach by backing away and ducking and weaving.

'Come here, you stupid horse!' Ros growled at him menacingly. She knew she was on the verge of losing her temper; which, she realized, would be fatal.

He splashed away again and Ros began to despair: a horse that was determined to keep out of your range could usually succeed. Even if he didn't tear away across the countryside he could still do himself a lot of harm: there

24

could be all manner of dangerous refuse on the floor of the pond. Her own plight wasn't something she thought about: it didn't really matter to her that anyone watching might think she was looking distinctly stupid. But then, out of the corner of her eye, she caught a glimpse of someone moving on the opposite side of the pond. Mrs Angela Sagaro had stepped through the gates and was watching everything that was going on.

Ros swore for the third time that morning. It was an even stronger word than the first she'd used. But she kept it under her breath. Now it was even more important to grab hold of Star. If she failed, her job in the stable would surely be over. Mrs Sagaro didn't make allowances for incompetent people. She simply got rid of them.

As Star delayed fractionally before moving again, Ros moved as swiftly as the water would permit. She lunged for the reins – and succeeded in getting her fingers round them. Star, of course, tried to back away but Ros refused to let go, even though initially she was pulled off her feet and collected another soaking. Alexander's Star shook his head vigorously from side to side but he couldn't shake her off.

'Got you, Star!' she exclaimed thankfully. Somewhat to her surprise the horse then capitulated, permitting her to lead him straight out of the pond and on to the lane, almost as if he had taken note of Mrs Sagaro's headmistressy attitude and decided not to offend her further.

'You were plainly being rather stupid, Rosalind,' Mrs Sagaro greeted her coldly as Ros led the horse towards the gate.

'Sorry,' Ros said, determined not to start shivering in spite of the chill that was seeping into her bones. 'It was, er, a complete accident.'

'How did it happen?' Mrs Sagaro demanded. She was always ruthless in her cross-examinations; and her cross-examining technique ought to have been the envy of ambitious barristers.

'Well, er, I just forgot that Star liked water so much, that he'll always amuse himself in the pond if he gets half a chance. Sorry.'

'But what were you doing riding him? I assume you *were* riding him before all this nonsense happened?'

'Oh yes. Tony – er, Mr Vasson – well he wanted to ride Mantola so he asked me to swop. So I did. I mean . . .'

She meant that she had no option but she couldn't say that; Tony's sister would simply insist that *of course* she shouldn't have handed over her horse to anyone else, whatever the orders or blandishments. Her job was to look after Mantola *at all times*. She had no business even looking at another horse. Ros had heard all that sort of thing before. Now she flicked a sideways glance at Angela Sagaro, noting the coiffured elegance with not a single hair out of place, the haughtiest of expressions, the fingers tapping on the cordless telephone she carried whenever she was away from her office (it sometimes rang in the stables while she was attending to a horse but the tone was so mild no horse was disturbed by it). At the moment anything could be going through her boss's mind but Ros didn't have any doubt that it concerned her own future at Tildown House.

'What have I told you always to do, Rosalind?' Angela Sagaro asked with a menacing softness in her voice.

'Just to obey your orders, Mrs Sagaro, nobody else's.'

'Exactly! But, of course, that's too much to ask, isn't it? Too much for a girl with a mind of her own, like you. *Isn't it*?'

'I've *said* I'm sorry, Mrs Sagaro. It won't happen again, I promise.'

'That it won't! You can be sure of that. I'll tell you this, you wouldn't have forgotten anything about your beloved Mantola, would you? Oh no! If you know that he hates water, why can't you remember that Star loves it? Rosalind, I've told you before and I'm not going to go on telling you. At Tildown House you've got to think of *all* the horses, not just those that are your favourites. *Every* horse here is special and has got to be treated as special.'

She paused but Ros knew that wasn't to allow an interruption. Angela was simply gathering up her thoughts for the next onslaught on her victim. But this time she changed her point of attack.

'That horse needs to be dried off, so see to it without further delay, young lady. Then I want you to see to The King. He needs a bandage on that near-fore tendon. And I want it done in the next few minutes, not at the end of the day. Understand?'

'All right. But can I, er, get some of this pond water out of my clothes first?'

Mrs Sagaro managed to look thoroughly pained (as perhaps she was). It was clear she was near the end of her tether, as she expressed it from time to time. 'Surely, *surely* I don't have to tell you that the horses come first, come before everything. And definitely before your *own* comfort. They can't bandage themselves, you know, but you, well, *you* can attend to your own little problems whenever you have a moment to yourself.'

It was only what Ros had expected but she was beginning to feel chilled as well as distinctly uncomfortable with all that water seeping through to her skin. It wouldn't have hurt Angela to offer to see to Star herself. But, of course, she wasn't the sort of woman who would do a job, except in an emergency, which she was paying someone else to do.

So Ros led Star past the cool scrutiny of the proprietress of Tildown House Stables and into the yard; Star by now wasn't at all excitable and she was thankful for that. If the horse had tried to play her up she was sure she'd have lost her temper; which would been fatal. By now Mantola had been returned to his box, from which he was watching her intently, and there was no sign whatsoever of Tony Vasson. Doubtless, she surmised, he'd gone into the house to make himself some breakfast or cadge it from Angela's housekeeper. Naturally he hadn't thought to put a rug over his mount, let alone brush the mud off his hocks. In Tony's view, that's what girls were for.

As briskly as possible she sponged and dried Star, trying not to think of her own discomfort. Lydia would probably have offered to help if she hadn't been equally busy with her own horses. 'Now, behave, will you, after causing all that trouble,' Ros told Star severely as she left his box. She guessed he was impatient for his breakfast but he'd have to wait a little longer for that.

King Perusa, a chestnut with three white socks and a decidedly uncertain temperament, was a horse she often looked after (Star was really in the charge of a girl called Anne-Marie who was attending a wedding in Morayshire). His leg troubles seemed to be worse, and occur more frequently, than any other horse she had known. Yet his ability on the track was such that his owner and trainer wanted him patched up whenever possible so that he could 'win just one more race'. Yet when he did record that victory, the sequel to which was another bout of leg trouble, they always insisted on keeping him in training 'for just a little bit longer to see if he can do the trick for us again'. The horse didn't really have any bad habits and it was only occasionally that his temper flared up; but Ros had never taken to him and never accorded him any of her spare time as she did Mantola.

'Be with you in a minute, Manty,' she called as she hurried into King's box with the strong-smelling liniment for his leg. The chestnut backed away, his eyes rolling.

'Oh come on, this is just the usual stuff, so stop making a fuss,' she told him.

Like most horses (and human beings), King Perusa usually responded to a kind voice and praise; but Ros wasn't in the mood to soften him up before putting the bandage on. He was wasting her time and she resented it. The way things were going she'd never get to school today.

Well, it wouldn't be the first time she'd been absent because of her work at Tildown House, but she wasn't anxious to upset Mrs Andersen at present. She needed her year-tutor's support if she was eventually to get a place at college.

It took a bribe in the form of a carrot she'd been saving for Mantola to secure King's co-operation. Even then he practically stamped on her foot twice. She was just completing what she thought was a highly satisfactory bit of medical treatment when she heard again the dreaded voice of doom.

'For goodness' sake, Rosalind, surely you don't think *that's* the way to do it, do you?'

Slowly, Ros straightened up. Her temper, she knew, was on the edge of blowing up. From the moment she'd arrived at the yard that morning things had gone wrong; nothing at all seemed to have gone right. She was chilled to the bone, she was hungry, she was missing her time with Mantola: and now Angela Sagaro was finding fault after fault with her. Swearing wasn't enough to release her emotions: she wanted to lash out and hit somebody or something. If she bottled everything up much longer, then . . .

'I asked you, Rosalind, a *question*. Please have the courtesy to answer it.'

Ros chewed on the inside of her lip, working out what to say; but instinctively her free right hand was stroking King's neck, damp with perspiration from his worries about his latest medical treatment. Although Ros would never be aware of it, it was her obvious affection for the horse that saved her from losing her job at Tildown House. Mrs Sagaro's patience, never one of her strong suits, had almost been eroded on a day that had begun badly for her, too: two of her trainers who regularly sent horses to be cared for had decided to place them elsewhere in future because their owners were keen to cut expenses.

'I'm sorry, Mrs Sagaro, I don't see exactly what's wrong. I

think I'm a bit upset at the moment, so I'm not seeing straight, I expect.'

Ros's coolness surprised Mrs Sagaro as well as herself, though Angela had no idea of the effort involved in presenting such an attitude.

'Two things, two very obvious things, I should have thought. One, that the bandage isn't straight. Bandages, as I've told you and the other girls times without number, are worse than useless when they're wrinkled. They can cause more trouble than they're designed to prevent because the flesh can be pinched and damaged under those wrinkles. And two, *never* tie the bandage on the tendon because to tie there is to place extra strain on the tendon itself, the very part you're seeking to help heal. You tie it on the opposite side of the leg to the tendon. Had you forgotten that?'

'No, Mrs Sagaro, of course not. I told you, I'm just, well, not at my best this morning. Sorry. It won't happen again.'

And, before another word could be uttered, she bent to ease away the wrinkles and retie the bandage where it could do no harm to that vital tendon, always so slow to heal because of a poor blood supply to the surrounding area. Tendons were the subject of more lectures than any other part of a horse's anatomy and Ros had even drawn diagrams of them several times to improve her understanding of their importance. Located behind the cannon bone (the equine equivalent of the shinbone in humans) the tendon, no thicker than a man's thumb, but three times the length, took all the pressure of the horse's half-ton weight when the foot touched the ground. So it was little wonder that the tendons of racehorses, so much involved with sheer speed, should always require the most delicate attention whenever they were inflamed or strained.

'It won't happen again, I can promise you that,' Angela said as coldly as before. For a few moments she watched in silence as Ros briskly dried King with the dry rubber and then, with sweeping circular arm movements, brushed

30

him, sleeking him down before putting on his rugs again and methodically fastening all the straps. Angela didn't miss a single movement and Ros was conscious of her scrutiny; but then, it was nothing new. She had a habit of keenly watching everything a new girl did to make sure everything was done according to her detailed instructions.

The feed was already prepared but Ros cut up some dandelion leaves and mixed them with grated carrot to add flavour to King's meal. Then she filled the buckets with fresh water before presenting her employer with a dazzling smile (and Angela would never know the effort that had cost, either). 'May I look after Mantola now, Mrs Sagaro?' she inquired with immeasurable politeness.

But she had to wait for an answer. At that moment the telephone rang in Angela's hand. For some moments she simply listened in silence to whatever was being said; and then, very matter-of-factly, she started asking questions.

'Where do you say it is? Oh yes, Sharrock Hill. Yes, I know that. Just beyond the Grey Mare pub, second on the right, sharp rise. Yes, I've noted all that.'

So she had, on a notepad attached to the underside of the instrument: an invention she said she ought to patent.

'Well, all right. See you then. Oh, hope so. Thank you for calling.'

She looked rather bemused and Ros didn't know whether to repeat her own question. Every minute that passed she was feeling colder and more uncomfortable. As she glanced down at her feet she saw that water was still dripping from her clothes and forming a small puddle on the concrete.

'Bit odd that,' Angela remarked, as much to herself as to her solitary listener, it seemed to Ros. 'Fellow wants me to see this horse tonight. Seven thirty. No other time will do. Seems to think Tildown is the only place that can restore this invalid to real fitness. Flattering, I suppose, in a way.

31

But I was hoping to get some book-keeping done tonight. Never enough time in the day for that job.'

'Oh,' said Ros, not really interested in Mrs Sagaro's business or social arrangements for the evening. 'Well, I was asking whether I could go and see to Mantola now.'

She received another of those familiar calculating looks and it was a moment before she got her answer; quite plainly, Mrs Sagaro was still reflecting on the phone call.

'No, not immediately,' she said with sudden emphasis. 'You must be thoroughly chilled and I don't want you catching your death, not in my stable!'

Ros was staggered. Was Mrs Sagaro actually making a joke, or an attempt at a joke? That was practically unheard of. But her attitude had quite definitely changed in the last few moments.

'So, go and run yourself a bath, there's plenty of hot water. Use my bathroom. Put your things to dry in the airing cupboard on the landing. Oh, and there's a towelling robe behind the bathroom door. You can use that.'

'But – but – I mean, Mantola . . .'

'Lydia can see to him. Won't break her back to add to her workload, just for this once. She gets off pretty lightly most of the time.'

That's not what Lydia thinks! Ros told herself. Lydia was forever complaining about the extra jobs Mrs Sagaro piled on her without warning or, worse still, any recompense in the form of more money or time off in lieu. If only she could find congenial work in another stable, Lydia threatened, she would leave here without a second thought. But Ros suspected that she didn't really look very hard; Lydia was the kind of girl who always needed to grumble about something to help her through the boring parts of her routine.

'That's very kind of you, Mrs Sagaro. Thanks a lot. I'll be as quick as I can.'

'Oh, take your time, get yourself warm again. I'll talk to you later.'

Although Tildown House, low-ceilinged and rambling, wasn't especially impressive, the bathroom was nothing short of luxurious in Ros's opinion. She'd visited it only once before and not to have a bath, either. Pink was the predominant colour and the tiles, reaching to the ceiling, were floral-patterned. Even the towels, large and fluffy and sensually soft, were pink.

Ros turned both taps on and then quickly stripped off her thoroughly damp clothes; the towelling robe was where it was supposed to be (Angela was too well organized not to have put it back where it belonged) and so she slipped it on to take her clothes to the airing cupboard.

'Oh bliss, bliss, perfect bliss,' she murmured as she subsided below the water level and the warmth enveloped her. Because the taps were in the middle of one side she was even able to choose which end to rest her head on a sponge support. Suddenly, her day was beginning to improve. She sank a little lower in the water and began to think about how she would make up for her neglect of Mantola when she came in the following morning. She had just decided he should have half a bottle of his favourite tipple, a beer with a particularly strong flavour, poured over his main meal of the day, when she became aware of some commotion in the yard. The bathroom window – one of the few in the house not double-glazed – opened on to the yard but Ros wasn't inclined to leave the comforting water to see what was going on. For once, somebody else could sort things out. Even Tony Vasson ought to be willing to help in a real emergency. Except that no doubt he'd find some excuse to disappear.

'Rosalind, ROSALIND! I need you immediately. Now, at ONCE!'

'*Unbelievable!*' Ros told herself, half rising from the water. 'She can't just change her mind like that!'

But, as she'd learned, sometimes to her cost, in the months she'd known her, Angela was quite unpredictable.

33

With her, today's positive ambition was on tomorrow's reject pile. Hastily, Ros stepped out of the bath, pulled the admired towelling robe over her shoulders and cautiously peered out of the window. Lydia was the first person she glimpsed, half-sitting, half-leaning on a low pile of hay bales; Lydia clutching her right arm just below the elbow; Lydia in obvious pain, white-faced and dazed of expression.

The only reason Angela wasn't continuing to yell for Ros's assistance was that she was speaking into her telephone with an urgency she seldom displayed. Ros wanted to ask what had happened but she sensed that Lydia was in no position to reply to a shout from an upper window.

She dried herself off as best she could in twenty seconds and then dashed to the airing cupboard for her clothes which were still almost as damp as when she'd taken them off. Leaving her underwear to continue drying she tugged on jodhpurs and sweater, wishing that Angela had been decent enough to offer her a change of clothes to accompany the generosity of the use of the bath.

'There's an ambulance on its way – be here in no time, they said,' Mrs Sagaro announced just as Ros reached the yard, having seen no sign of Tony in the house.

'But Lydia, what's wrong?' Ros asked.

'My own fault, really. Got my elbow smashed,' Lydia told her gaspingly. 'Stupid, really. I just sneezed. Couldn't help it. All that dust hanging about. And Mantola just moved.'

Ros stared. It hadn't occurred to her that Mantola might be responsible for Lydia's misfortune. 'But – but he didn't knock you over or something, did he?'

Lydia shook her head. 'Wasn't his fault, Ros. I expect the sneeze startled him. It was pretty loud. But I had the brush in my hand at the time, just reaching up to his shoulder. He sort of skittered sideways. And I was rammed into the wall. Well, my elbow was. Must have cracked it. Sounded like it.'

'Is it terribly painful, Lyd?'

'Yes.'

It was the awful simplicity of that answer that revealed how much she was suffering. Ros wanted to put her arm round her friend but she realized that wasn't wise: if the bone was broken then she might compound the damage.

'Could be the shoulder, you know – collarbone,' Mrs Sagaro suggested. 'I know it's painful but it's soon mended. Most jump jockeys break a collarbone at least once a season. Soon get over it, matter of days sometimes. Then they're riding again with no ill-effects.'

Only some of that was true but neither Ros nor Lydia felt like disputing it; in any case Angela, they recognized, was trying to be comforting.

'Can I get you anything, Lyd?' asked Ros, feeling helpless.

Lydia shook her head again, the pain now making her feel thoroughly sick.

'Look, Rosalind, you'd better see to the horses,' Mrs Sagaro said crisply. 'I'm sorry you didn't get a proper bath. But the horses must – '

' – come first,' Ros completed the sentence for her resignedly.

But before she could move, an ambulance swung through the still open gates and into the yard. Lydia surrendered herself to the men's ministrations and Ros was impressed by the gentle way in which they attended to her injury.

'Is it broken then?' Lydia asked wanly.

'Can't say yet, love. They'll have to have a proper look at the hospital. But don't worry, you'll survive. I swear to that. Nothing that can't be mended. Now, if you'll hop in the back – well, with a bit of help from my mate, that is . . .'

'Shouldn't someone go to hospital with her?' Ros asked, looking directly at Mrs Sagaro. 'I mean . . .'

'I'll be fine, Ros, honest,' Lydia insisted. 'You and Mrs Sagaro have enough to do. Then you've got to get off to school, right? Look, everything'll be OK.'

35

'Well – '

'Look, it was my fault, my own stupid fault,' Lydia went on. 'Don't blame Mantola.'

'I wasn't going to,' Ros said softly as the ambulancemen closed the rear door.

'Well, we could have done without that little incident,' Mrs Sagaro remarked unnecessarily as the ambulance departed. 'I'm afraid this will mean rather a lot more work for you, Rosalind, if you can possibly spare the time. Will you be able to come in this evening, after school?'

'I expect so, but I must go and see how Lydia is first. I mean, she might be out of action for ages and need things doing for her.'

'Of course, of course,' was the smooth response. 'We must do whatever we can for her. But Rosalind, if you could just see to the horses now as quickly as possible . . .'

Mantola seemed quite unaffected by the trauma that had occurred in his box and he snuffled into her palm the moment she swung the door open. This time, though, he was out of luck. King had already consumed Mantola's titbit.

'Well, there is one thing, Manty,' Ros told him as she completed the brushing Lydia had started. 'They say bad things always happen in threes. And I've definitely had my three already this morning. That bruise from the rake. Getting chucked into the pond by Star. Then having my bath interrupted and having to do extra work. To say nothing, come to think of it, of Tony Vasson pinching my ride on you. Yes, I reckon I've had all my bad luck for a whole *month* rolled up into one bit of a morning. So things should start to improve any moment now.'

In the days that followed Ros Hayward was to remember that remark; and wish with all her heart that she'd never uttered it.

Four

That evening Ros was deeply immersed in *Madame Bovary* when the telephone rang. Reluctantly she put down Flaubert's novel and wondered whether to answer it. She was sure the caller was her mother, detained again in London. Well, it was already late enough for her to have gone to bed so she could always claim later that she was asleep.

Even as she lifted the yellow receiver from its wall bracket she was still undecided whether to speak; she could leave it off the hook and then her mother would at least know she was at home. That was all that mattered. She put the receiver almost to her ear.

'Rosalind, I want you over here as fast as possible,' were the words she heard. She didn't need to be told that the caller was Angela Sagaro. That crisp, authoritative tone was unmistakable.

'What! But what for?' This sort of summons had never happened before and Ros couldn't believe that Angela expected her to work her third shift at the stables that day.

'We have an emergency on our hands and I need you over here immediately. There's no point in discussing things on the telephone. So hurry – '

'But Mrs Sagaro, it's so *late*. I mean, I was practically on my way to bed and – '

'Mantola's missing. We don't know what's happened to him nor where he is.'

It was the most stunning news she'd ever been given.

'So you'd better hurry, Rosalind,' Mrs Sagaro added in a softer tone. 'You're the one who knows him best.'

'I'll be there as fast as I can make it,' Ros promised. She charged upstairs to pull on jeans and sweater; there'd been no chance during the day to wash the clothes muddied by the pond and the sight of them on her bedroom floor was a reminder of what a terrible day it had been. Surely it couldn't go on like that?

She was through the garden gate and swinging herself back into the saddle of her racing bike when she remembered that she'd not locked the back door; if her mother returned home during her absence and discovered that unsecured door there'd be trouble of a different order. Not to be risked. Swiftly she returned to the house and locked up.

During the eleven minutes she spent on the journey (she'd never known what her record was for the trip but this night she established a new one) her mind was in such turmoil that she could make no firm guess about what might have happened to her beloved horse. But wherever he was, she would find him. Of that she *was* sure.

All the horses were looking out of their boxes in their usual inquisitive fashion when she arrived at the yard; all except Mantola, of course. Instinctively Ros crossed to his box. The door was open as if to underline that he wasn't there. But before she could explore the box for clues Mrs Sagaro emerged from the house. As usual, she was clutching her telephone as though it were a talisman.

'Still no news, I'm afraid,' she announced without any smile of greeting. 'I've rung all my neighbours but no one's seen anything. They've said they'll keep a look-out in case Mantola turns up in their yard or garden or whatever. Somehow I don't think there is much chance of that.'

'But how could he just disappear? I mean, wasn't he bolted in when you finished evening stables?'

Although she'd never been a trainer herself Mrs Sagaro

followed the customary racehorse trainer's practice of visiting all the horses in the middle of the evening to ensure that all was as it should be with each of them; in racing circles that was always known as evening stables.

'Of course, and I'm positive he was completely secure. It's a complete mystery. Absolutely astonishing.'

Ros didn't really know what to ask next. It would be easy enough to make accusations about carelessness but, of course, Mrs Sagaro was her employer (well, if not in a legal sense, in every other way). In any case, Angela prided herself on her efficiency and normally that efficiency couldn't be faulted.

'It would never have happened, you know, if I hadn't gone on that wild goose chase,' she was murmuring, almost to herself. 'Utter waste of time. And now this . . .'

'What wild goose chase, Mrs Sagaro?'

'Oh, some chap rang me up this morning – in fact, I think I was here in the yard at the time. And you were here, too. Must have been about the time of your little swim in the pond. Well, anyway, he wanted me to look at some horse – good one by all accounts – that had been giving him a bad time. Been scared stiff by a beating from an Irish jockey, so he claimed. Wanted me to consider trying to get the animal back to normal. He made a real song-and-dance, the chap who rang, I mean, about my being there this evening about seven thirty. Then, when I got there, no one knew a thing about him. Couldn't find any clue to man or horse. Utter waste of time.'

'Was it a – oh, what's the word? Yes, a malicious call?'

Angela stared at her and then carefully ran a finger round her lips, one of her mannerisms when provoked into reviewing a situation she thought she controlled. 'I truly hadn't thought of that, Rosalind. But, yes, I suppose it could have been. I mean, when I got there – Sharrock Hill, that is, just beyond the pub, the Grey Mare – nobody had even heard of this chap, Williamson, he said his name was.

Ordinary sort of name. That's why it never occurred to me it could be, well, some stupid sort of hoax. But he was so positive about the location, and the farm he described simply doesn't exist. I just assumed I must have got the address wrong after all.'

She looked so taken aback that Ros hesitated to ask her anything else. It was just an idea – an absurd one, she supposed – that popped into her head that there could be something funny about an invitation to a remote spot at a precise time in the evening.

'What on earth made you think of that, Rosalind?' Mrs Sagaro wanted to know.

Rosalind shook her head, as baffled as her employer. 'Just struck me as odd, that's all. In fact, you said yourself it was odd when you took the call. It was just after you talked to this man you said I could have a bath.'

'Ah yes, but, well, what would be the *point* of it, that's what I can't grasp. Seems an absurd thing to do, unless . . .'

'Somebody must have wanted you out of the way,' Rosalind declared, having rapidly worked it out. 'Anybody who knows Tildown House knows that Mrs Barnes finishes her housekeeper duties soon after seven and you're the only one on the premises. Normally, I mean. So if you're out . . .'

'True,' Angela agreed. 'But we come back to the main point. Why would someone do that, get me away from the house?'

'So there'd be nobody to stop them from stealing Mantola! It has to be, hasn't it?'

'But why Mantola? And who, *who* would want to do such a vile thing?'

Ros had no answer to either of those questions. She didn't really believe someone had stolen her horse but the evidence, such as it was, pointed that way. Mantola could not have got loose on his own; and, even supposing he had, why wasn't he somewhere in the vicinity of Tildown House? Because there could be no reason for him to wander far from home, where he was well fed and well looked after day and night.

'I'm going to ring the police,' Angela announced. 'They've got to be told, anyway. I hadn't thought of doing it right away. I mean, some motorist might come across Mantola, wandering across a lane or main road. Frightful thought.'

While she made that call Ros went into Mantola's box. But it looked as it always did when he wasn't present. There were no signs of any disturbance such as might have occurred if someone had tried to take away the horse by force. It defied belief that anyone should want to steal Mantola. He certainly wasn't exceptional in any way as a racehorse and his training problems (those frail legs that were so easily jarred by excessive work or hard ground) ensured that he always needed time to recuperate after a severe race. If the person who'd stolen him didn't realize that, then Mantola would soon be useless to them if he was worked too hard. Ros had heard about illegal racing, either in the depths of the country along hidden lanes or makeshift tracks on remote moors; but she'd never met anyone who'd actually witnessed such events. Perhaps it was just typical stable talk in an industry that thrived on rumour and tall stories.

One possibility she had to admit was that he had been kidnapped in order to sell him abroad. British racehorses which hadn't reached top rank and therefore wouldn't be valuable as stallions were often in demand among foreign buyers who would pass them on to trainers in their own countries where standards of racing were not nearly so high as those in Britain. If that was the case then she'd never see him again – *unless* they could find him before he was put on a ship (only the élite of the racing world went by air). And tracking down a stolen racehorse was a job only the police could properly handle.

She wandered across to the tack room to check whether the thieves (by now she was convinced Mantola had been stolen) had taken his saddle or anything that was exclusively Mantola's. But she had to use her set of keys to unlock the door and there was no sign that force had been used to get into the room where all the stable's equipment was stored. Nothing, so far as she could tell, was missing. The saddle he'd worn that morning was exactly where she'd left it. Lingeringly she fingered the headband Mantola so often wore. Was that going to be her only souvenir of all the love and care she'd lavished on him? Ros felt the tears start in her eyes and she had to brush them away as Angela appeared at the door.

'Found anything?'

Ros shook her head. 'Nothing's been taken that I can see. And the door was locked. Was – was Mantola's box open, by the way? I mean, he could – '

'No, closed – but not bolted. Which could mean anything, I suppose. But, thinking about it, I agree it looks more likely that *someone* pushed it to after Mantola went.'

'Are the police coming to investigate?' asked Ros as she closed the tack room door.

'Well, I think so. Frankly, they didn't appear to be greatly interested. I suppose if I were reported as having a defective tail-light on my Range Rover they'd be round here like a shot to cart me off to jail!'

'But they *are* coming?'

'Well, I believe so. I told them, I've never been so surprised in my life as when I opened Mantola's box and discovered he was missing. Couldn't credit it. Thought for a moment you must have put him in a spare box for some reason. But, of course, I'd seen him in his own box at evening stables . . .'

'What made you look for him in the first place?'

'Pure accident. When I got back from that wasted trip to Sharrock Hill I glanced round the yard as I usually do, to see everything's as it should be, you know. I felt that something wasn't quite right. Couldn't put my finger on it at first. Then I realized what it was. That light above the feed room. It was on.'

Ros looked puzzled. 'But nobody ever puts that on, do they? I mean, with the switch in that stupid place next to the first box where No Ticket is.'

'Precisely. So I guessed somebody had been fiddling about – wouldn't be you or Mrs Barnes. So somebody had been in. Thought it must be one of the village children, just wanting to have a look at the horses perhaps.'

'Possible, but unlikely. I mean, they've never done that in the time I've been coming here.' Ros paused. 'But why *would* anyone put that light on? Nothing's gone from the feed room, has it?'

Angela shook her head. 'Definitely not. No, I suspect whoever's been here was simply checking on each of the boxes and therefore switched on that light by mistake. They wouldn't remember that light wasn't supposed to be left on. After all, we do have other lights on to illuminate the yard at night.'

'But you didn't just switch it off. You went round and looked in all the boxes?'

'Rosalind, I do try to be efficient, you know,' Mrs Sagaro pointed out with a theatrical sigh. 'I mean, I know I leave a lot of the routine duties to you and Lydia, and all the domestic tasks to Mrs Barnes, but I think I can claim to be methodical in what I do. I have my owners to think about, you know. What's more, switching off lights is important with electricity the price it is. You'll soon find that out when you have a home of your own. Anyway, I decided to check that all was as it should be, looked in each box – and discovered Mantola was absent. Quite a shock, *quite* a shock!'

'Sorry, Mrs Sagaro,' Ros mumbled. 'I wasn't making a criticism, just wanting to know really why it's all happened. I still can't believe anybody would – '

But she stopped as a police car swung into the yard and drew up beside them. The first thing that occurred to Ros was that the blue light on the roof wasn't functioning. So presumably the police hadn't hurtled to the scene, eager to solve the mystery they'd been presented with and catch the culprits without a moment's delay. That view was endorsed by the rather languid way in which the uniformed sergeant got out of the driving seat and put his cap on. There was no one else in the car.

'Evening,' he greeted them in the same unhurried manner. 'I gather one of your horses has got away.'

'Well, not on its own, if that's what you're thinking, officer,' Mrs Sagaro replied with a hint of reproof in her voice.

'Sergeant, ma'am, Sergeant Northgrave, actually,' he told her matter-of-factly. 'Oh, and I've heard all the jokes anybody could make about my name.'

'Sergeant, I wouldn't *dream* of being facetious about anybody's name. I can assure you I have enough trouble with my own. Now, I presume you want to have a look round and check on things for yourself?'

To Ros it didn't appear that he had any intention of checking on anything that wasn't absolutely essential; already he seemed thoroughly bored with the Case of the Missing Racehorse, as Ros was headlining it. Sergeant Northgrave wasn't a local man; or if he was she'd never seen him before. She'd never have forgotten anyone so amazingly thin and tall. He gave the impression he could pass through a keyhole without touching the sides. Perhaps his thinness counted against him where energy was concerned and that was why he was so lethargic.

'Well, I'll do what's necessary,' Sergeant Northgrave

44

conceded in answer to Angela's question. 'I suppose you've looked in all the places this horse could be, have you?'

Angela stared at him as if she couldn't believe what she'd heard. 'There aren't many places, sergeant, where a full-grown horse could hide himself in a stable of this size,' she told him with chilling logic, just keeping the sarcasm out of her tone.

'If a monkey wants to hide, the best place to do it would be in a monkey house,' Sergeant Northgrave declared imperturbably, reciting a dictum one of his superiors believed in implicitly. 'So a missing horse is most likely to be found with other horses. What I'm saying, madam, is this: could the missing horse be in one of the stalls along with another horse, the regular inhabitant of that stall, if you take my meaning?'

'I do take your meaning, sergeant, and the answer is still no. Mantola is definitely not on my premises wherever else he might be. I've checked very thoroughly. That's the first thing I did when I knew he was missing.'

The sergeant nodded in the approved thoughtful-detective fashion. This was no more than he'd expected, though sometimes members of the public could be quite stupid when something was thought to be stolen. They'd panic and fail to search the most obvious places. 'Well, have you contacted all the people who live round here to see if the horse has wandered on to their property? At night they may be unable to see him – you did say he was a dark-coloured animal, didn't you?'

By now Mrs Sagaro was unable to conceal her exas-peration. She hadn't expected Sherlock Holmes but she had hoped for someone with some deductive skills and imagination. 'Yes, he is a dark horse and – oh, no pun intended, I assure you!'

But, as she and Ros saw, Sergeant Northgrave hadn't thought it was; he remained as impassive as his name.

'Yes,' Angela went on, 'a bay. Look, I can show you a horse of similar colouring.'

She drew the sergeant in her wake to Alexander's Star's box; and Star obligingly turned round in his own length as if aware that he was being scrutinized for the purpose of helping the police with their inquiries into his stable companion's disappearance.

'Yes, I see,' the sergeant said unhelpfully. But he didn't, Ros noted, write anything down in a pocket book; she'd supposed all policemen did that when they were involved in an inquiry. But he did ask another question. 'If the horse has been stolen – and, of course, that remains only a possibility – there could be other reasons why he's not here – well, then I expect someone would have been sniffing round first to see the lie of the land before making a move, if you follow me.'

'I think I do, sergeant,' Mrs Sagaro replied with a resumption of her very cool manner.

'Well, then, I was wondering if anyone – well, suspicious-looking – any suspicious characters have been observed in the vicinity lately. Anyone come to mind, madam?'

'Now you mention it, there was something a bit odd, a bit out of the ordinary,' she related. 'Mrs Barnes – my housekeeper – well, she had a visitor the other morning. Chap who said he was marketing a new feed for racehorses. Asked if he could see our horses, claimed he could tell whether they were in prime health just by looking at them, by the shine of their coats. Well, that's a lot of nonsense, really: I mean, *anyone* can judge by the bloom on a horse's coat whether it's fit or not. Doesn't need an expert. And in any case, sometimes that's misleading. I mean, a horse may *look* fit physically but you can't tell if it's mentally fit. And much of our time here is spent on repairing the psychological scars that racehorses have picked up. So – '

'But this man who called allegedly about feedstuffs?' he interrupted politely.

'Oh yes, sorry! Well, Mrs Barnes formed the distinct impression that he was just being nosy, that he wanted to see what was going on in the stables. Actually, there's nothing unusual in that. Members of the public who back horses have their own favourites and sometimes turn up to ask if they can see them, give them a Polo mint or some titbit like that. As long as there's nothing suspicious about them we usually let them have a quick look, though we're very careful about titbits. In racing, you can't be too careful.'

'So what happened next with this man who turned up and said he was in feedstuffs?' Sergeant Northgrave was now demonstrating patience and genuine interest. Ros was beginning to think he wasn't quite such a hopeless type after all.

'Well, she told him – Mrs Barnes did – that we had our own regular supplier of all the feeds we need. So that was that. He cleared off.'

'Did Mrs Barnes see him leave?'

Angela looked surprised. 'Well, I've no idea. I don't suppose she deliberately watched to make sure he was off the premises. She has enough to do, getting on with her own work. She's my right hand, is Mrs Barnes. Well, in the house that is. Anything else I can tell you?'

'I don't think so, thank you, madam. I'll be getting off home. Nothing more that can be done at this end.'

'But aren't you going to take fingerprints or anything like that?' Ros blurted out, unable to believe that a police investigation into stolen property could be so perfunctory.

'I really don't think that would be helpful, miss,' the sergeant told her with the first hint of a smile on his face. Until that moment he'd been so lugubrious that Ros had supposed he was incapable of ever believing that anything in life could be amusing. 'Very likely there are *hundreds* of different prints on the walls of a place like this. Couldn't possibly sort out any new ones. Anyway, professional thieves generally use gloves – don't leave anything to chance, those beggars.'

'Oh, so you think Mantola *could* have been stolen, then, not just wandered off for a little walk on his own?'

The sergeant's eyes narrowed as if he were playing the detective's role in a local rep production. 'There's quite a trade in horseflesh these days, miss. Finish up as steaks in French restaurants in Belgium, some of 'em. Others are used to feed all manner of other animals – dogs, mainly.'

Ros suddenly felt sick. Just because he thought she was being sarcastic – and she was not – he'd retaliated by being as offensive as possible. Surely no one would steal Manty just to kill him for – for pet food . . .

'Sorry, miss, didn't mean to upset you,' the sergeant resumed, trying to make amends. 'But that reason's as likely as any other for the horse's disappearance, I'm afraid. Goes on all the time. Only thing that makes me think possibly it isn't, is this chap saying he's in the feedstuffs game. I don't suppose you've seen any suspicious characters around the place? I'm assuming, by the way, you're employed here.'

'Rosalind is still at school but she works for me whenever she has free time,' Mrs Sagaro explained. 'Mantola is her special responsibility when she's here. In her eyes he's a very special horse. Rightly so.'

It was while Mrs Sagaro was speaking that Ros suddenly remembered the man who'd been watching Mantola on the gallops. Did he come under the heading of suspicious characters? She had no idea but it seemed best to mention him.

'You never said anything about this to me, Rosalind,' Mrs Sagaro said sharply.

'Didn't think it was important enough to mention to anyone, until now,' Ros told her apologetically. 'I expect he was just interested in picking up some tips for future winners.'

'There're always men up on the Downs, watching the horses,' Mrs Sagaro explained.

'Better than watching young girls – young people,' the sergeant remarked.

'But it's unusual for someone to be standing on a *car* to get a good view – and Manty seemed to be the only horse he was interested in,' Ros persisted. She'd now convinced herself that the tout was at least partly responsible for the disappearance of Mantola. And if he was on the criminal side of racing at least that meant he wouldn't be dealing in dead animals.

'Did you get a good look at the chap?' the sergeant wanted to know.

'Sorry. I was riding past him, remember, so all I got was a fleeting glimpse. But he was wearing a green trilby. Can't be many of those about, can there?'

This time Sergeant Northgrave actually managed a grin. 'You'd be surprised,' he said.

That was virtually his parting shot. They would hear straight away, he promised, if the police had any news; but they weren't to hold out much hope if the horse didn't turn up in the next twenty-four hours. Conversely, they were requested to phone the office immediately if the horse turned up of its own accord or a neighbour brought him back.

'Honestly, I don't know what we pay our taxes for if that's all the help we're to expect,' Angela remarked as the police car was reversed out of the yard. 'Must be the sort who doesn't like horses: probably frightened by one as a child and never got over it.'

'But what are we going to do if the police aren't looking for Mantola and nobody else spots him?' Ros asked. She feared that Angela, too, might lose interest if he wasn't found soon. After all, she had plenty of other horses to command her attention.

'It's what Sir Alan's going to say that's worrying me,' Mrs Sagaro admitted. 'I mean, very wealthy men can be very stingy when it comes to losing something, you know. Especially if it's not their fault.'

Ros wasn't going to confess that what worried her, apart from the whereabouts of Mantola himself, was the chance of losing a ride in the Midthorpe Marathon. But she couldn't believe that Manty wouldn't reappear in the next few hours.

'I'm not going to tell him until I have to,' Angela went on, referring to the owner. 'There's no point in worrying somebody unnecessarily. Things may look quite different in the morning. Rosalind, dear, do you think you could just stay a few minutes and help to settle the other horses? All this disturbance in the yard isn't doing them any good at all.'

If she'd been on her own Ros would have switched on her cassette player and placed it in the middle of the yard; at full volume it could produce a very loud sound indeed. Brahms and Mozart and Simon and Garfunkel had a soothing effect on the horses, in her experience, while a rousing Rossini overture was guaranteed to gee them up first thing in the morning (though not many horses were slothful at that time of day, anyway). Angela, however, didn't really approve of such 'novelties', as she described the introduction of music into the yard. It wasn't banned; but it wasn't encouraged. Normally she looked favourably on any genuine experiments designed to help in the rehabilitation of the patients, as she was inclined to describe her horses. After all, they were often sent to her because more conventional methods of treatment in other establishments had failed to provide a cure. But she was against anything that seemed to her to be aimed at 'humanizing' the horse. It was one of the few points on which Ros disagreed with her.

So now, as she made her final round, topping up water buckets, freshening hay nets, changing a salt lick, she had to rely on honeyed words where a calming influence seemed necessary. But her mind wasn't on such routine tasks; all she could think of was Mantola and what might be happening to him at that moment.

'Do you *really* think he's been stolen?' she asked Angela when they'd finished their rounds and, rather to her surprise, she'd been invited in to have some coffee.

'I can't think there's any other explanation, Rosalind,' admitted her employer, looking as doleful as Ros felt. 'Why they should have wanted Mantola I can't imagine. Maybe they just wanted one horse, *any* horse, for their purpose. He is placed near the entrance, isn't he? And because I have to run everything on a shoestring and can't afford the luxury of late-night security systems, well, it's as easy as falling off a horse to steal one from us!'

Ros didn't know how Angela could make jokes, even feeble ones, at such a time. 'It's a bit odd about that chap coming to sell special foods, isn't it? I mean, he *must* have been sussing the place out. Wonder if he came back when you and Mrs Barnes weren't around or didn't see him. I mean – '

'Well, if he did perhaps Lydia saw him, perhaps she even spoke to him,' Angela suggested. 'Lydia doesn't always remember to pass on messages, you know, so she's quite likely to have forgotten to mention any visit like that.'

'Hey, I've been forgetting Lydia!' Ros exclaimed. 'Wonder how she's getting on with her injured elbow. Oh, that's awful, I should have dropped in to see her.'

'And I should have telephoned her but it went clean out of my mind with all this carry-on at Sharrock Hill and now Mantola's disappearance. Maybe I should ring now – '

'Don't give it another thought, Mrs Sagaro. I'll drop in on my way home. You know it's almost on my route. Then I can see how she is *and* ask her if she has any ideas about,

51

about what's happened this evening. Look, I'll go now, shall I? I mean, if there isn't anything else you need me for?'

'Oh, I wish you would, Rosalind – call on Lydia, I mean. That'll ease my conscience. Look, take her these grapes. They're what invalids are supposed to have, aren't they?'

She took a sizeable bunch of black grapes from the fruit bowl and found a plastic bag for them. Ros, eager to get away, looped the bag round her wrist before speeding off across the yard on her bike. Her one worry now was that Lydia would be in bed, fast asleep, and her mother would refuse to let Ros see her. Everything probably depended on how much pain she was in and what treatment the hospital had ordered.

It was Lydia herself who answered the front door bell. Her mother, she said, was out baby-sitting for a neighbour.

'But how are you?' Ros wanted to know, eyeing the sling supporting the right arm. 'I mean, shouldn't you be in bed, resting, getting your strength back and all that stuff?'

'Probably, but it's a bit awkward lying down with your arm all tied up like this. Painful, too. I mean, it's in a splint so that's a problem for a start. I felt a bit groggy after the anaesthetic but that's cleared up now.'

'How long will it be before it's, well, cleared up?'

Lydia shrugged and then winced. 'They never know that, do they? Probably at least a fortnight. The nerve was affected, that's why there was a lot of swelling. And the humerus was damaged. That's the funny bone, in case you didn't know. And no jokes, thank you very much!'

'Wasn't going to make one, Lyd. I'm too – sad, for that. Absolutely ripped up inside, to tell the truth.'

'Something else is wrong, apart from my accident, right?'

Ros handed over the grapes, telling her to make the most of them; it wasn't every day that dear Angela handed out free gifts to her staff. It suddenly didn't seem fair to burden Lyd with the bad news about Manty; but then, she would have to hear it from somebody . . .

'Oh, crikey, it really hasn't been your day, either, has it? Especially after the dire Tony took Mantola from you and then you got a ducking in the pond. And I thought *I* was having a bad time,' Lydia sympathized, offering her friend a grape.

'But why him, Lyd, why *Mantola*? I know he sends me into ecstasies but that's only because he's special in my life. I have to admit that he's not the world's greatest racehorse. He's not won the Derby or any other top race. Nobody knows whether he'll be a successful sire. He's got dodgy legs and a bit of a temperament. So why take *him*?'

For a moment or two Lydia, sucking the juice from another grape and thinking, didn't answer. 'Well, I suppose there's only one answer: it was a mistake, Ros.'

'Meaning?'

'What I say: they meant to take another horse but kidnapped Mantola by mistake.'

Ros stared at her friend. 'Which horse?'

'Alexander's Star, I imagine. It was when you said about Angela telling the cop that Mantola was a dark horse and then showing him Star. Well, then it clicked. I mean, they *are* a bit alike, aren't they? And if the kidnappers aren't terribly clued up on horses generally they could easily have mistaken Mantola for Star.'

Now it was Ros's turn to stay silent for a few moments while she considered the implications of that idea. It did, she couldn't deny it, make sense. Star was the sort of horse who would be attractive to kidnappers who either wanted a ransom for him or planned to sell him abroad where his speed might win him many races.

'Another thing I've just thought of,' added Lydia, now in inspirational form. 'If that guy on the gallops this morning *was* one of the thieves and he'd been told to look out for the horse Tony Vasson was riding, well, he would assume that Mantola was Star, wouldn't he? Tony's ridden Star a lot lately. The gang have probably got a good sort of spy network and they'll know Star's nearly fully fit again.'

Ros nodded. 'It all fits,' she agreed. But then another thought struck her. 'But what will they do when they discover that Mantola isn't the horse they were after? I expect they have some way of identifying Star from photos or his racing passport.'

Lydia didn't reply. Suddenly she busied herself in the kitchen, putting the kettle on to make another cup of coffee. Ros followed her and repeated her question. Lydia swallowed. 'Well, they're not going to bring him back, are they? Hand him over and say, sorry, we just made a mistake, took the wrong horse. Are they?'

'No, of course not. So – well, what?'

'Well, I think they'll just have to cut their losses. Do it the easiest way so they can't be traced.' She paused as she saw the bleak look on Ros's face. 'I think they'll kill him. Ros, I'm sorry, love, but honestly that seems to me the logical thing for them to do. To destroy the evidence of the crime, you see.'

Five

One week later there was still no news of the whereabouts of the missing racehorse. Ros felt by then that she was the only one who cared about the fate of Mantola, though Mrs Sagaro from time to time admitted that she was still 'very upset about the poor horse'. In Ros's eyes, she didn't look particularly upset; she seemed to have got over the loss of one of her patients remarkably quickly. No doubt that had something to do with the fact that Sir Alan Needwood, Mantola's owner, had promised to send her another horse to look after, saying he didn't blame the stable in the least for the theft of Mantola. The nicest thing that had happened to Ros in a very long time was that Sir Alan had sent her a personally written note sympathizing with her over the loss of 'her charge', as he put it, and hoping that Mantola would soon be found so that she could take part as planned in the Midthorpe Marathon. She thought he was the kindest and most thoughtful person she'd ever met in her life.

So far as she knew, only one newspaper had reported the mysterious disappearance and that story was contained in a single paragraph; there was no description of Mantola and so no one reading it would feel they could help to find him, however hard they looked. There had been no return visit by Sergeant Northgrave or any other policeman and when Mrs Sagaro, prodded or needled into action by Ros, telephoned to see if there was any news, the formal reply was the familiar 'the police are pursuing their inquiries'. Where they were pursuing them, and in what fashion, they declined to say; the stable would be informed as soon as there was anything to inform them about. End of message.

'We've got to do *something*,' Ros insisted, refusing to accept Lydia's view that Mantola had probably been disposed of by one means or another.

Lydia, back at the stables and working one-handedly on a part-time basis because she said she couldn't bear to be idle, offered a variety of suggestions, none of which Ros thought was particulary practicable.

'Honestly, we might just as well stare into a crystal ball,' she said scathingly.

'We could do that, if you like, if you think it would help,' was Lydia's unexpected response to that sarcasm. 'I mean, there's a woman over at Ditchburnham who actually does do crystal-ball readings, or whatever it's called. Must be a bit like a TV set in a way. So I suppose it could be called screenings! We could pop over and see her.'

Ros didn't say anything for a moment. She wasn't sure whether she believed in the supernatural or the possibility of receiving messages from beyond the grave or anything like that. But her grandmother – and in the last couple of years of Gran's life she was very close to her – used to tell her stories about how *her* mother had foretold the death of a child in a horse-riding accident and a train crash in which several people were injured. Gran didn't think she'd inherited her mother's powers but from time to time she said she could read what was in someone's mind; and when she was positive about it then invariably she was right. 'Lindi-love' was what she always called her granddaughter and she loved her very much; so she would talk to her for hours about everything under the sun. There was a line from Shakespeare she loved to quote whenever the topic of metaphysics was under discussion: 'There are more things in heaven and earth, Horatio, than are dreamt of in your philosophy.' Ros had once looked up the quotation and found it came from *Hamlet* and a scene deeply concerned with ghosts and spirits and subjects that troubled the mind. Ros had accepted her grandmother's belief that not everything could be explained away in purely practical terms. Sometimes a special kind of faith was the guide you needed to overcome difficulties; but that faith wasn't really any kind of advertised religion. It couldn't be thought of in those terms. But it had a real power of its own, Gran declared. And Ros believed her.

'Do you know her, then, this woman with the crystal ball?' she asked Lydia who was becoming rather bored by this repetitive conversation.

'Well, I have met her but it's Mum who knows her best. I'm sure Mum would fix it up for us to go over there if you want to. It won't cost a fortune. I mean, she doesn't charge a proper fee – money – but I think she expects a present of some sort, something that she can use. Mum'll know what to give her.'

'Does she see pictures in this crystal ball, you know, pictures of people she's interested in?'

'I expect so, Ros. But I told you, I don't know the details. You can only find out by going to see her, can't you?' Lydia, suspecting that a crystal-ball screening might be altogether more interesting than anything currently available on the family television, had delayed switching the set on. 'Anyway, what've you got to lose?'

'Maybe she can't, well, *communicate* with animals. Perhaps all her pictures are of people.'

'Oh, I don't think so. No, definitely not. Old Mrs Simpson went to consult her about her pet budgie which had flown away when its cage was left open. I seem to remember Agatha was able to help her in some way, though whether the budgie ever turned up again I don't remember. Look, give it a try, Ros. I'll get Mum to fix it up. D'you want to go tonight if she's, er, available?'

'*Agatha*?'

'Agatha Elliott, that's her name. Look, are we going or not?'

'OK.'

Lydia, eager for any new activity after so many days at home with little enough to excite her, dashed into the kitchen to fix things up.

Her luck was in. Her mother was already intending to visit a friend in the village on the other side of Ditchburn-ham and so would be happy to give them a lift; and Mrs Elliott needed no special pleading to agree to receive the girls within the hour. Lydia's mother rummaged in a cupboard and handed over a long, slim box of scented soaps, an unwanted Christmas present of some vintage.

'Here,' she said, 'you'd better give Agatha these and some chocolates – she prefers soft centres. Then she'll do her best for you. Hope everything works out, Ros.'

Mrs Elliott's house was on the very edge of the village, a cottage painted all white with a black studded door and a shining brass knocker shaped like a blacksmith's hammer.

Ros was surprised when the door was opened to them. She'd expected the woman to look like a witch. Yet nothing else in Ros's life at present was normal so really it should have been predictable that the woman didn't match the image she'd had of her. It was only the name that was out of the ordinary. Agatha. The sole Agatha she'd ever heard of was the famous writer of detective stories and Ros sup-posed that was a pen-name anyway. This Agatha had a chubby face, spectacles that glittered with semi-precious stones when caught in a certain light and hair piled in a bun on top of her head. Ros thought she looked as though she ought to be behind the counter of an old-fashioned wool shop.

'You're not expecting miracles, are you, child?' she greeted them, staring rather fiercely at Ros, who hadn't been called 'child' by anyone for years.

'Well, no – I mean, yes!' Ros replied, uncertain what was

the true answer. A miracle was really what she hoped for, because how else was she going to find Mantola?

'Most people come here expecting miracles and go away disappointed,' Mrs Elliott declared, looking now most definitely disapproving. 'But miracles just aren't on, not with me. Mine is the scientific approach.'

Ros was already beginning to feel disappointed. She suspected Mrs Elliott might turn out to be as ordinary as her second name and her appearance. Lydia, she sensed, was eager to say something but Ros wasn't going to encourage her. It was a pity she'd ever listened to Lydia in the first place. Instead of wasting her time in the dark with Agatha Elliott she could have been doing something positive to find Mantola.

'Perhaps you'd be good enough to take your place round the table in this room,' Mrs Elliott was now inviting them, in a distinctly formal manner.

'Thank you very much,' said Ros politely and followed Lydia into a dimly lit front parlour (that was the only word that seemed to her to describe the claustrophobic room dominated by a round rosewood table, polished so that it gleamed, on which stood a glass ball atop a pyramid). Thick curtains concealed the only window and on the walls hung several pictures of windmills. On a glass-fronted cabinet, of the kind used to display best china, was a ceramic model of yet another windmill, this one complete with sails and even a tiny weathervane. Was Mrs Elliott simply addicted to windmills in the way that some people collected china ornaments? Or did they in a mysterious way help her to make contact with whatever she was looking for? Ros supposed it was possible. Anything might be possible with a woman like this, who was so ordinary in every way, apart from believing herself to possess extraordinary powers.

'Please be seated,' she said in the same cool manner, indicating that Ros should take the high-backed chair opposite the door with Lydia sitting on her left. Lydia's attitude had changed. Now she was subdued, almost nervous, as though she sensed that something unwelcome was about to happen. Ros wanted to smile to reassure her but she couldn't manage it. The atmosphere in that room was having a worrying effect on her, too.

Mrs Elliott closed the door behind her with care: the sort of care a jailor might give to a cell holding a desperate escapologist. Then, to Ros's amazement, she began to seal the space between the door and jamb with adhesive tape. Was that to keep them in or to keep baleful influences out? Ros didn't dare ask. She didn't want to be rebuffed again. Her one concern now was how long this ordeal would last. She had no belief at all that she would learn anything that would lead her to Mantola or give her hope that he was still alive.

Before sitting down opposite her two visitors Mrs Elliott dimmed the light above the table and then, for several moments, simply sat in silence as though she were either praying or waiting for inspiration. Ros felt a tiny shiver pass along her spine and she held herself rigid to prevent her reaction being obvious. Could it be that nothing was going to happen, that they would sit silently until Mrs Elliott announced that she could do nothing to help? Why wasn't she asking them questions about their wishes?

'Tell me, child, what are your hopes?' she asked suddenly in a voice now sepulchral and much as Ros had expected it to be.

'That you can help me, us, to find a racehorse that's been stolen from Tildown House, Mrs Sagaro's stables,' she said nervously. 'It's a dark bay horse, very nearly black really, called Mantola. I work at Tildown House and look after Mantola. He means – well, nearly everything to me.'

Mrs Elliott nodded as though that were exactly what she wanted to know or even had been expecting to hear. At that moment she was looking quite steadfastly at Ros as though weighing her up. Ros, a trifle embarrassed as well as nervous, switched her own gaze to the sphere of crystal but it looked precisely as it had a minute ago. But she realized she couldn't see what Mrs Elliott might be seeing on the surface that faced her; and that, Ros presumed, was where the vision would appear if it appeared at all.

'Do you have any idea at all who may have taken the animal, or where he might be? However vague your ideas.'

'Afraid not,' Ros admitted.

Mrs Elliott nodded. It was what she'd expected. But there was something else. 'Do you possess any object, anything at all, which has been attached to the horse? I realize you won't have brought with you any reins or a saddle or anything of that nature. Still . . .'

'Ros, you've still got that ring, haven't you?' Lydia asked eagerly. She felt she had been on the sidelines too long and was in danger of being ignored completely. 'You know, the one you wove out of hair from Mantola's mane.'

'Oh yes, of *course*.' Ros dug into her jacket pocket and produced the ring which fitted her middle finger. 'I, er, made it myself but I don't wear it all the time because I'm afraid of losing it. You know, if I take it off and put it down somewhere and then forget to pick it up. Also, I don't know that it'll last for ever if I keep it on all the time.'

Mrs Elliott held out her hand and, reluctantly, Ros passed the ring to her. She didn't examine it but simply folded her fingers over it as though she were never going to let it out of her grasp.

'I want you to think, think as hard as you've ever thought about anything in your life,' she said in a voice that was barely audible. 'Think about this horse, think about this horse. Picture it in your mind. Picture where he is now, where you think he may be. Think. Think.'

Ros noticed that Mrs Elliott closed her eyes as she spoke; and that made her wonder how on earth she was going to see anything in the crystal ball. If, that is, anything were going to appear there. But she felt she should do as ordered.

61

It was easy enough: Mantola was in her mind's eye all the time. But where he was she could not imagine.

'Are you thinking of this animal, too, Lydia?' Mrs Elliott suddenly asked sharply.

'Oh, er, yes, of course,' Lydia replied, guilt evident in her tone.

'Then you must think harder, my dear. *Harder*.' As an injunction it was kind but firm.

For several more moments nothing at all was said and Ros found herself listening to Mrs Elliott's slightly raspy breathing. It was becoming an eerie experience in this now over-heated room with a woman who might be anything: a genuine medium who could get in touch with another world; or a charlatan. Yet what had Mrs Elliott to gain from leading them into a new belief, except a box of scented soaps and some sweets (which she didn't yet know she was going to get)? It could only be that she wanted to give some significance to her otherwise drab life; if, in fact, her life was drab. But . . .

'I see a horsebox, a very old style of horsebox,' she announced unexpectedly, cutting right across Ros's meandering thoughts. Mrs Elliott's voice was now crisp, almost excited: and with the loudness of confidence.

Ros sat up and stared at the crystal ball but it appeared no different from a few moments ago. Or was there a tinge of colour, a sort of clouding effect? It wasn't possible to be sure but Ros believed there'd been a change. Certainly there'd been a change in Mrs Elliott, now staring at the crystal with the intensity of a magician being shown a wonderful new trick.

'Is there –' Ros started to ask until Mrs Elliott silenced her with one movement of her hand in the air. Ros glanced across at Lydia: but Lydia was as riveted by the sphere as their hostess and wasn't ready to communicate about anything. Suddenly, Ros noticed what appeared to be pinpricks of light within the ball: and she was positive they

62

hadn't been there moments earlier. Now she glanced round, trying to discover whether they could be reflections of any lighting in the room.

But the room was lit by just the one dimmed bulb in the ceiling. So, if they weren't reflections, where had those lights come from? Ros glanced back at Mrs Elliott whose concentration hadn't wavered: she was still studying whatever she could see in the depths of the ball in the centre of the rosewood table.

'I see lights, small lights, not powerful lights,' she announced with that sudden certainty that made it all sound so surprising. Ros was strangely pleased. So she could see what Agatha Elliott herself could see!

'I see candles – yes, candles – lanterns, too. Perhaps.' For the first time there was a note of doubt in Mrs Elliott's voice. 'Yes, I am sure, lanterns. In a great room, a *huge* room.'

Ros frowned. How on earth could she tell, from a sphere as small as that, what size a room was? It didn't seem likely, not likely at all. She wanted to ask questions but sensed that wouldn't be welcome. So she must wait until Mrs Elliott had seen all there was to see.

'I see a man with a hammer, a hammer raised high.'

Ros, as she heard those words, felt a chill within her: a sharp sensation of horror and helplessness. Was Mrs Elliott witnessing Mantola's . . . *death*? She shuddered, unable to control her emotions.

'Is it –' she started to ask in spite of her recognition that she shouldn't speak. But another raised hand stopped her.

'It has gone now,' Mrs Elliott said very matter-of-factly about a minute later. 'You may ask your questions now, child.'

Ros swallowed, almost unable to say what was in her mind. The candles and the lantern worried her. They sounded vaguely religious and it flashed through her mind that such lights might appear at a funeral or be used to

63

illuminate a death scene. She knew all that was fanciful, probably quite stupid, but it was in her mind.

'Do you think the hammer – a weapon – was it anything to do with – with *killing* a horse?'

'I doubt it,' Mrs Elliott replied in a businesslike voice. 'It was quite a small hammer, the sort auctioneers use. What's it called? Oh, a gavel, I seem to recall. Much more like that.'

'And the lights,' Ros started again tentatively. 'You said there was a big room. Do you suppose it was a church, a cathedral even?'

Mrs Elliott appeared to be considering the point. 'No,' she declared eventually, 'it was bigger than that. Wider, anyway. It wasn't a properly constructed building at all. Quite unusual.'

'What do you think the candles and the lanterns mean?' Lydia inquired hesitantly.

'It is not my task, my way, to interpret the pictures I see,' Mrs Elliott replied in a return to her formal manner. 'I can only tell you what I see, not what is meant. And what I see may not be relevant to your needs at all. I told you to expect no miracles.'

Ros nodded. She wondered why Mrs Elliott bothered to look in the crystal if she couldn't understand what she saw. But, still . . .

'Can – can anybody see the pictures, what you see, in the crystal, Mrs Elliott?' she asked, wondering what sort of response that might evoke. It might be regarded as exceedingly impertinent.

Mrs Elliott, however, simply smiled. 'If you possess what I call "the switch". The scenes are always there. But, like a television set, it has to be tuned in to the proper channel. Unlike a television receiver, the channels in the mind of the user are not always clearly marked, they are not as obvious as a switch on a wall.'

Ros didn't know what to say to that, so she said nothing. At that moment she had no idea at all whether she'd learned anything useful. She would go away and think about it and discuss it with Lydia, who was looking as baffled as Ros felt. There was just one glimmer of light, nothing to do with either candles or lanterns, and she wanted particularly to think about that. But she had one more question to ask first: 'The horseboxes you saw at the start, Mrs Elliott. You said they looked very old. Could you, well, describe them a bit more than that? Were they any special colour, could you tell?'

'Oh, let me think.' Mrs Elliott closed her eyes and plainly concentrated. 'Well, they were sort of oval in shape, with ribbed walls, not a bit like the modern horseboxes I see around the village. Those ones are like small bungalows on wheels, aren't they? No, these would be big enough for one horse, perhaps two at a pinch. Oh, and one had a sort of little door at the front, a bit like a wicket gate, if you know what that is.'

'Never heard of that,' Ros said.

'Oh, well, it's a little gate set in a big gate, to save opening the big one when perhaps only one person needs to come through. Well, this horsebox door was very like that, just for a person, and that person would have to stoop, too.'

'So it was very old, this van?'

'I should think so. Except that the paintwork was quite bright, very fresh, just as if it had recently been repainted. But that's easily done, isn't it, slapping a new coat of paint on something to make it seem quite new?'

Ros, exchanging a swift glance with Lydia, experienced a tingling sensation between her shoulderblades. So she really had learned something after all. Well, she hoped she would be able to follow up this clue and then . . .

'But you didn't see anything of Mantola? You know, *my* horse – well, you know what I mean?'

Mrs Elliott was shaking her head. 'My guidance to what I am seeking comes in many forms, child. It is rarely as clear as – as a photograph. One has to learn to make some interpretations. And now, if you'll forgive me, I am feeling a little tired. The degree of concentration that is needed is very – taxing.'

'Oh yes, of course. Sorry. Er, Lydia, have you . . .'

'Oh yes.' From somewhere within the depths of her anorak Lydia produced the gifts for Mrs Elliott, who was now unsealing the door so that they could return to the normal world. 'Thank you very much for helping us so much. We hope you'll enjoy these little gifts.'

'How *very* kind, Lydia. And, child, I do hope you will be successful in your search. I am sure you *deserve* success.' Then Mrs Elliott handed back the precious ring she'd been clutching all the while.

Ros wasn't at all sure how to take that remark but her one thought now was to talk with Lydia. She was thankful that Mrs Elliott didn't try to detain them with offers of tea or other refreshments. After emphasizing how grateful they were for Mrs Elliott's efforts on their behalf, the girls left. So as not to risk disturbing 'your mysterious conclave', as she'd put it, Lydia's mother had said she'd await them in the car park of the White Hart (so if she wasn't in the car she'd be enjoying a little refreshment!).

'It must be one of Phil Swift's, mustn't it?' Ros said eagerly as soon as the cottage door closed behind them.

Lydia didn't need to be told what Ros was talking about: often enough they'd commented on the habit of the owner of Bennet's Farm of buying up ancient, sometimes completely antique, horseboxes and 'doing them up' for resale at a handsome profit. A neighbour of Mrs Sagaro's, Mr Swift described himself as a gentleman farmer, which meant that he didn't do much work himself. Even when he got another horsebox he couldn't bring himself to paint it himself: he actually employed a professional housepainter to do the job. Not for nothing had the girls christened him 'Idle Jack'.

'Must be,' Lydia agreed now. 'But what's the significance, Ros? I mean, I expect Mrs Elliott has seen plenty of those boxes in her time. But why should they suddenly turn up in her crystal ball?'

Ros shrugged. 'Dunno. But it must mean *something*, Lyd. Something to do with Mantola.'

They paused outside the entrance to the pub car park, each striving to make sense of what they'd heard. Then Lydia asked tentatively: 'What do you think about the hammer, Ros? I mean, I could tell you were worried about it. So was I.'

'Much harder that, isn't it? I mean, it seems so *violent*. Though it doesn't have to be. Could be somebody just, well, constructing a loosebox or something.'

Lydia nodded. 'I thought that! Some form of shelter, anyway. First I thought about a coffin, but that's daft. They don't put horses in coffins, do they?'

Somehow Ros managed a wry grin. 'Very comforting that. Thanks!'

'No, Ros, I didn't mean anything wrong! I was trying – '

Ros gave her a hug and a kiss. 'I know you were! I'm only joking. Glad I can manage to. I have a funny feeling, though, that Agatha has got something right for us. Don't know what, but – something.'

'Oh great,' said Lydia, sounding thoroughly relieved. 'Look, I think Mum's spotted us. We'd better go and tell her the news. She'll be dying to know.'

'I've made a decision, anyway,' said Ros, only half-listening to what Lydia said. 'Tomorrow I'm going to see Phil Swift. I've no idea what'll happen but I'm convinced I'll get something out of him. I've just *got* to.'

Six

Lucky it's Saturday, Ros told herself as she swung into the
lane leading to Bennet's Farm (*Private Road: Strictly No
Trespassers, No Parking, No Turning* – that was what the sign
said and Ros knew it meant that young people weren't
welcome at any time to stop under the sheltering trees
while they kissed and whispered and made dangerous
plans; and which, defiantly, many did, until they were
spotted). Because it was Saturday she wouldn't have to
furnish explanations to Mrs Andersen about why she'd
missed another half-day's attendance; and, more import-
antly, she could act immediately on last night's impulse to
ferret some information out of Jack Swift. Of course, he
wasn't called Jack at all – that was simply to suit the 'Idle'
description – but Phil, which she thought was just as bad. It
meant he had the initials P.S., which was almost as funny,
as an afterthought; or perhaps it was like Psst, meaning,
Hey, I've something to tell you.

Ros didn't know why she was in such a frivolous mood
because, frankly, there was nothing remotely funny about
the reason for her visit to Bennet's Farm. If she didn't gain
some useful information then she would be lost; she had no
idea at all where to look next in the search for Mantola. So
she had to make sure Phil Swift treated her inquiries with
the utmost seriousness.

Because the farm (no animals were kept there, no crops
were harvested) was close to Tildown House, she was

familiar with the vehicles the Swift family used and she was relieved to see that all of them appeared to be parked on the cobbled forecourt of the pink-washed house with the leaded windows and carriage lamps beside the door. So there was a good chance that Phil Swift was at home. The bell made an appropriate ding-dong noise deep inside the house and mentally she rehearsed the first question. But his greeting was such that it went straight out of her head.

'Ah, hello, young lady,' he said in a rather leery voice. 'You must have read my thoughts. I was going to phone you up today. Terrific that you've come round instead. Much easier to talk. Come in.'

So, dazed, she followed him across the impressively large hall and down a narrow corridor. He was taller than he'd seemed from a distance, but then she'd usually seen him sitting at the wheel of a car or striding away with a gun under his arm. The beard concealed the thinnesss of his chin and perhaps compensated for the small amount of hair (artificially black, she guessed) on top of his head. His office was where they were heading but, naturally, he described it as his study.

'Got a horse for you to ride, if you're interested,' he told her when, rather reluctantly, she sank into the soft leather armchair he indicated.

Her heart leapt. Surely he couldn't have – have *found* Mantola for her? That would be incredible. Yet –

'You look flabbergasted, darling. No need to be, I promise you. I can't guarantee it'll give you a good ride or even a safe one.' And he laughed as he said that.

So he was talking about a completely different horse: and her heart resumed its normal place. She was even able to think about the oddity that nobody these days seemed to use her real name when speaking to her (Mrs Elliott's preference for 'child' drew from Lydia's mother the explanation that Ros had 'a look of youthful innocence'; which made Ros laugh. Phil Swift's use of 'darling' was all too plainly an affectation: he would address any half-attractive young female as darling without a moment's thought.

'For a moment I thought you were referring to Mantola, that you'd *found* him for me – for us,' she said when it became necessary to say something.

'Mantola?' His surprise seemed quite genuine.

When he assured her that he didn't know what she was talking about she explained what had happened, adding that she'd hoped he might have some information about the theft or the whereabouts of – she stressed the point – Sir Alan Needwood's horse.

'All news to me, dear,' he said dismissively. 'But then, you see, we've been away. Soaking up all the old sun in Martinique – that's in the Caribbean, you know. So a bit out of touch with *local* happenings.' He paused and flashed a kind of conspirator's look at her. 'It's also the reason why I've not been able to get in touch – er, yes – get in touch with you before today about this ride I've got for you in the Ladies' Open at High Chance tomorrow. I mean, you're not riding anything else in the race, are you? That would be a bit of bad luck for me, wouldn't it, after asking you!'

'No, no I'm not,' she answered hastily before he could think of withdrawing his offer, an offer as welcome as it was totally unexpected.

It seemed an age since she had ridden in a point-to-point although, in fact, it was only a few weeks ago. Nowadays her main interest in horses was concentrated on working at Tildown House, but she'd always relished the excitement of the racetrack, even when the quality of the racing was as moderate as the events usually were at High Chance. In any case, the circuit itself was unusually stiff, with several of the fences cunningly constructed on slopes, some up, some down. Perhaps it was the formidable nature of those obstacles that deterred owners from sending their best horses to compete at High Chance. Ros had never won a race there but on several occasions she'd finished in the first four. In truth, none of her mounts had been much good at point-to-pointing: they were either simply too slow or unable to jump properly.

'Good!' Phil Swift exclaimed with apparent pleasure at her availability. 'I was very impressed the last time I saw you there. You finished third on a geriatric grey that thought it was a bulldozer! That's how it treated the fences, anyway.'

Ros laughed. That really was a very fair description of old Tankerton, the horse she had ridden for Mrs Leatherbarrow, a friend of Angela Sagaro's. Even Mrs Leatherbarrow herself, a forthright lady who ran an agricultural feeds business almost single-handed, admitted that her horse tended to live up to his name. Just by staying in the saddle for the entire race, Ros had greatly impressed her, she said. Unfortunately, Tankerton had soon afterwards begun to exhibit breathing problems and his owner retired him.

'So what's the name of this horse you want me to ride?' she asked, gaining the impression that perhaps she'd been a bit unkind in her judgement of Phil Swift. He was really quite nice when he smiled like that and his laugh was very genuine.

'Ah, this is Saskia Sound. A – '

'Oh, that's nice! I think it's important for a horse to have an attractive name. Some owners choose the most dreadful names like – well, Henry Humbug or Bit of Fluff or Itsagiggle. No wonder they're never any good, the horses with those names, I mean. Seems they know exactly what they're called and they *hate* it.'

'Well, I'm glad you like Saskia Sound as a name, but I don't know if she'll live up to it in your eyes, darling. To be frank, she's a bit of an old woman. You know, got a mind of her own. Only likes to do her own thing. Doesn't like being pushed around. But has ability, oh yes. No doubt about that. When she wants to show it. *When*.'

71

'Oh, another of those,' sighed Ros. 'I've had plenty of experience of horses like that, Mr Swift.'

'Phil, love, Phil – much friendlier.'

Ros wondered if he was on the verge of making a pass at her as he leaned forward across his desk but probably that was just his normal manner. There were quite a lot of men about who thought that every young girl should be friendly towards them in all circumstances.

'Is she, er, your horse?' she asked, deliberately refraining from using his name. In any case, in racing it wasn't usual, to say the least, for jockeys to be on very familiar terms with their trainers, whom they invariably called 'Guv'nor', or owners, nearly always addressed as 'Sir' or 'Madam'. Some jockeys thought the whole thing old-fashioned in the extreme but still kept it up.

'Hell, no! Can't afford horses like this one! Real race-horse, Saskia was. Cost a mint, I gather, as a yearling. No, Ros, she belongs to a mate of mine, fella called Nigel Trent. You'll meet him tomorrow, of course.'

'Oh fine.' She expected him to tell her more about the horse and the arrangements for the day but suddenly he was looking over her shoulder, eyebrows raised. Ros turned and saw Mrs Swift in the doorway, a rather fixed smile on her round, rouged face.

'Hi,' she said offhandedly to Ros, much as another teenager might have done. 'Phil, are you going to be long? Giovanni's doing my hair at ten and he's not used to waiting, you know.'

'Oh, sure, Bel. Won't be a minute. Just about finished, haven't we, Ros? Ros here is going to ride Nigel's lovely old chestnut tomorrow. Great, isn't it?'

'Lovely,' said Annabel Swift in a meaningless tone and departed, pushing her blonde hair into the nape of her neck with the palms of her hands.

'Nothing else, is there, Ros?' he asked – and then remembered something. 'Oh yeah, getting to the course. Want me to give you a lift? No trouble, I swear.'

'That would be fine, thanks. I'd er, like to get to know the horse as much as possible before the race. So – '

'Sure, sure. Look, I'll pick you up a couple of hours before the first race is due, then we can all have some grub together, meet Nigel and all that. Don't worry, I don't think the grub will affect *your* weight, darling!' He laughed heartily and stood up to show her out.

'There is something else, though,' Ros said quietly but firmly. Obviously it had gone completely out of his mind that she had come to see him about something quite different from what had now been fixed up. 'You see, I wanted to ask you about your horseboxes – you know, the, er, rather stylish *old* ones you, er, collect.'

'Oh, don't worry your pretty head about that, darling. Nigel'll be taking his horse in his own – '

'No. I wasn't thinking about that. You see, well, it just could be that one of your boxes is connected with Mantola's disappearance.' Mentally she had her fingers crossed that he wouldn't blow up at what might be interpreted as an insult.

He simply looked puzzled. 'How d'you make that out?'

'Well, it's a bit complicated and I can't explain it very well. Sorry. But I was just wondering whether you lent one of your boxes to anyone recently, about a week ago. And whether it could have been used to transport Mantola. Perhaps by mistake, if you see – '

Phil Swift was shaking his head. 'Definitely not. Told you, we've been away for, oh, well over a fortnight. And, as far as I can remember, the boxes are just where I left 'em. So nobody's made off with one, with or without my permission. Hey, listen, darling, what's on your mind?'

Ros had thought very carefully what her answer must be to this inevitable question. It had to be convincing and it had to defuse any anger that might have arisen.

'Well, it's just that somebody mentioned that one of your boxes was, er, in the vicinity when Mantola vanished. So we wondered . . .'

Again he shook his head, though with a thoughtful expression this time. 'Can't understand that, sweetie. Could be one of my *old* boxes, you know, the ones I've sold. But they weren't sold near here, not by a long chalk. One went to Scotland, one to Ireland, another to London – right in the City, though I think that could finish up anywhere. So, well, a mystery, eh?'

'Yes, a real mystery,' Ros agreed. 'Well, if you think of anything . . .'

'Be sure to let you know. Naturally.' Quickly they reached the front door. 'Right, then, see you tomorrow. When I hope we'll have some winners to celebrate.'

'Hope so,' Ros agreed again, and waved cheerio.

But as soon as she reached the end of the drive it was Mantola, not Saskia Sound, which dominated her thoughts. Phil (formerly Idle Jack) Swift hadn't been any help at all in solving the mystery of Mantola's whereabouts. So she should be spending all her free time making more inquiries, not accepting a spare ride on an unreliable mare in a point-to-point. It was in her mind now to turn round and tell Mr Swift she wouldn't be able to ride Saskia Sound after all when, with a a beep-beep-beep of the horn, his BMW, conveying his wife at speed to the hairdresser's, swept past her and accelerated up the lane. She supposed the horn-blowing was a friendly signal.

Ros sighed and pedalled harder. She'd have to race tomorrow after all. She'd given her word and she never allowed herself to go back on that. She just hoped it wasn't all going to be a terrible waste of time.

Seven

It was a miserable morning. Rain overnight had stopped at dawn, though now there was a steady drizzle; and the mildness off the temperature had induced a clammy mist so that visibility in the valley was poor. When she got up, Ros's first thought was that the point-to-point meeting would surely be abandoned (if the stewards couldn't see the fences from their own elevated position they'd have to call it off). That was a decision she wouldn't object to at all. Instead she could spend her day making further inquiries about Mantola.

She made her customary Sunday morning telephone call to Tildown House to see whether Angela Sagaro was 'in desperate trouble' and therefore needed her services; but Angela, expecting visits from influential owners during the day, said she'd be able to manage very well on her own and, anyway, Ros needed her day off and ought to have a proper rest. She'd already forgotten that Ros had told her the previous day that she'd be riding at High Chance. Sadly, there was still no news of Mantola. Ros had the feeling that Angela had now just about written the horse off as an ex-patient and no longer her concern.

To take her mind off her worries until her chauffeur arrived ('He'd hate it if he knew I thought of him just as a chauffeur,' she grinned to herself) she once again immersed herself in *Madame Bovary* and shared the tribulations of Flaubert's heroine instead. To her surprise, Phil Swift arrived early, predictably enough signalling his arrival by beeping his horn imperiously until she appeared in the front doorway to acknowledge that she was aware of his presence.

'In winning form today then, Rosalind?' he greeted her breezily when she slid into the back seat of the white BMW. From Mrs Swift she merely received a glacial smile; if the smile had been warmer she'd have complimented her on her fetching new hairstyle.

'Do you think they'll race?' she asked, noting the lack of a 'darling' or 'sweetie' from him today.

'Oh, sure to. It's clear up on top, anyway. I phoned Nigel, who lives up in those parts. Bound to be a bit muddy, though.'

'Which means slippery for the horses,' Ros pointed out.

'Oh, you'll cope with that, no problem.' A man like Phil Swift never saw problems in jobs he didn't have to tackle himself. 'Nige reckons you're on a good thing if you can manage to strike up a decent relationship with the old mare. Says she's in good fettle and rarin' to go. Have to keep that information from the bookies, though! I really fancy a touch today.'

'Well, it usually takes at least a couple of rides before a horse and jockey strike up an understanding,' Ros pointed out cautiously. 'So don't bank on anything. Saskia Sound might take an instant dislike to my style, you know.'

'Can't believe that for a moment,' he replied instinctively; and would have added to that if his wife hadn't been sitting beside him with a disapproving look on her face.

Nigel Trent's information proved to be thoroughly reliable, for when they reached the top of the ridge on which the High Chance course stood there wasn't a sign of any mist, the drizzle had disappeared and there was even a hint of the sun somewhere above the clouds. But as soon as she stepped out of the car Ros knew what the going would be like: muddy was a distinct understatement.

'Right then, let's go and meet the man himself,' Mr Swift announced, leaving his wife in the car while he charged off in the direction of some marquees.

Nigel Trent turned out to be as small in stature as a professional flat-race jockey. Smartly dressed in the kind of dark brown overcoat known as a British Warm and favoured by a great many racing people, he had a brisk, businesslike manner and a very firm handshake. Instantly Ros thought of the phrase 'stands no nonsense' and, amazingly, moments later he was using the same phrase to her.

'You'll find old Saskia can be a bit of a handful but you must stand no nonsense from her,' Mr Trent said, narrowing his eyes and nodding his head very positively as he spoke. 'I can promise you one thing, though. She'll start all right – never failed since we did the umbrella trick on her.'

'Umbrella trick?' Ros and Phil Swift asked in disbelieving unison.

'Oh yes, very effective, that trick with any horse that's reluctant to start in a race or sometimes whips round at the off,' Nigel explained smugly. 'What you do is walk up behind the culprit with a big black umbrella, ready to snap it open the moment they start playing you up. Hate it, they do. So they always co-operate. Don't know why it has to be a *black* umbrella but it always seems to work.'

Ros smiled. 'I must tell Mrs Sagaro about that one! Could help to reform some of her uncooperative patients.'

'If it doesn't scare 'em to death first!' remarked Mr Swift.

Ros had been expecting to be introduced to her mount straight away but it turned out that the mare was always walked to the course from her stable by her lass because, as Nigel put it, 'there's no point in the expense of driving a box over'. So, after all, she wouldn't meet Saskia Sound until just before they were due to race. It was then that Ros would receive her final instructions from the owner.

After a picnic lunch in, and partly beside, the BMW,

77

when Annabel Swift suddenly became quite chatty and insisted on describing to her all the manifold delights of holidaying on a tropical island ('Chance'd be a fine thing!' Ros told herself), Ros said she'd like to have a wander round the course to familiarize herself with the positioning of the obstacles and the state of the ground and so on. By now, she said, a lot of the runners had arrived and she just might meet some old friends, perhaps even ex-patients of Tildown House.

'Oh, by the way, just remembered something, seeing that old horsebox trundle by,' Phil Swift called just as she was setting off. 'You know, after you'd said about one of my "specials" being seen when your horse vanished I went and had a look at the three boxes I've still got, just to make sure they were still there. Well, they were. But when I had a look inside I found something a bit odd in one of them. An old bandage, terribly smelly, horse must really have been suffering to have had that on! Looked as if it had teethmarks on as well, horse's teeth, I mean, not human! Can't imagine what it was doing there because none of my boxes has been used for transporting invalids. And I swear it wasn't there before we went off on holiday. I'm bloomin' particular about my boxes, you know: they've got to be absolutely spick-and-span. Untidiness is the sign of a disorganized mind and no businessman can afford that!'

Ros experienced a surge of excitement. Mantola had been wearing a bandage on his off-fore the last time she'd seen him: a bandage she, of course, had put there. And it would be smelly because of the special liniment with the secret ingredient that the stable's vet favoured. What's more, the teethmarks alone would almost certainly identify it as Mantola's because of his annoying habit of picking away at any bandage that was in the slightest way loose.

'That's fantastic!' she exclaimed, to Phil Swift's plain surprise. 'That means it probably *was* your box they took

Mantola in. I mean, sounds just like the sort of dressing I put on his leg. I'll be able to tell the moment I see it, though.'

'Oh,' said Mr Swift, his jaw sagging.

'Oh no! You haven't destroyed the bandage, have you?'

''Fraid so, darling. Couldn't have a stinking thing like that hanging around any longer. I chucked it on the bonfire. I was getting rid of lots of accumulated rubbish yesterday afternoon. So it's gone up in the proverbial smoke.'

Ros tried not to be too downcast. Just when it seemed that a real, and vital, clue was found it was snatched away from her. It underlined how rotten her luck was at present. Now there was no way at all of proving that the Swift horsebox had been used in the kidnapping of her horse.

'Sorry if I've let you down,' Mr Swift resumed after noting her disappointment. 'What I can't understand is why *my* horsebox should have been used. I mean, I now accept that it was very likely, from what you told me and the evidence of that old dressing which they must have over-looked when the horse was taken out. I mean, it doesn't seem to me to have any logic to it.'

Ros had been trying to work that out, too. 'Well, the only thing I can think of is that it means they didn't have a horsebox of their own. And they didn't know anybody they could borrow one from without arousing suspicion. Does that seem logical?'

'Definitely! Good thinking, sweetie.' He paused as an idea occurred to him. 'There is something else, too: they returned the horsebox, too, didn't they, so I reckon they didn't take it all that far. I mean, if they'd transported your horse hundreds of miles away they'd most likely just have abandoned the horsebox. Wouldn't have been worth their while, too much trouble, to bring it back. Does that seem logical to *you*?'

Ros brightened immediately. 'It certainly does, it really makes sense! If they'd pinched your box and abandoned it a long way off you'd've complained to the police and they'd've started a real investigation, and had a clue where Mantola might have been moved to. Are you going to tell the police about the bandage and our theory and so on?'

He frowned. 'I'll have a word with a chum of mine at County Headquarters. But somehow I doubt if they'll be excited about somebody borrowing the box, especially as we have no real proof. The police tend to like hard facts to go on, you know.'

'I do know,' Ros replied, thinking of the lethargic Sergeant Northgrave. 'Look, I'll have to go otherwise Mr Trent will be looking for another rider.'

'Well, best of luck, sweetie. Come back a winner and we'll all go home in pocket. And I'm sure Nige knows plenty of other owners with horses you could ride. Worth thinking about.'

There was time now for only a limited viewing of the course; she looked askance at the take-off area at the second open ditch and decided she really ought to get as near to the wing of the fence as possible. The fifth fence was a downhill jump and she'd have to be careful not to take off too soon. By that stage, however, Saskia Sound and she ought to have *some* understanding of each other and so she could coax the mare into doing exactly what was necessary.

'Riding a good 'un, are you?' inquired a female voice, breaking into her thoughts.

Ros turned to find staring at her a tall, well-built girl with a mass of curly dark hair and a round, attractive face: but the blue eyes were hard and unsmiling and she was slapping a whip against one jeans-covered thigh.

'Well, I don't really know how good my horse is because I've never ridden her before,' Ros admitted. 'What about you?'

'The favourite, probably: Time Trial. You'll know him, of course.'

'Er, well, yes.'

It wasn't really true. Ros knew a good deal less about

80

point-to-pointers than she did about horses raced by professionals on the flat and over hurdles. Time Trial was a name that must have been mentioned in her hearing but she couldn't remember any details about it. However, that didn't matter because Amanda Glossup, the girl she was talking to, soon enlightened her about Time Trial's wonderful abilities and his string of successes. Listening to the dedicated Amanda it was impossible to imagine their ever losing another race as long as they lived.

Ros would have preferred to continue studying the course entirely on her own but she couldn't shake Amanda off and so they made their way together to the marquees which did duty as offices and weighing-room and changing-rooms. During the walk Ros was relentlessly interrogated by her companion about her own riding record in point-to-points and her job at Tildown House; Amanda was quite amazed that she should accept a ride on a horse that was a completely unknown quantity but, she admitted, 'a ride's a ride, I suppose, and you never know your luck'. Ros agreed.

'I'll tell you one thing, though,' Amanda confided just before they went into the changing-room for lady riders, as it was described on a board by the entrance. 'Some of these girls are real cowgirls: ride like fury, trying to win at any cost. They'll give you no room when you need it and take your ground without a second's hesitation. Capable of anything if they're in with a chance of winning, or what *they* imagine is a chance of winning. So be ready to fight for survival!'

'Oh, I will, thanks,' said Ros, who suspected that for some reason Amanda was exaggerating the problems ahead of them. After all, there wasn't much kudos in winning a Ladies' Open at High Chance and the prize money was really quite risible.

The colours she was to wear rather appealed to Ros: yellow jersey with red spots, and black epaulettes and black-and-yellow quartered cap. They'd been chosen so that they could be seen from a distance and Ros knew she'd be under keen observation all the way. But, of course, that applied to every rider. There were eight runners and most riders seemed to know each other whereas Ros had met only two of them, and then only casually at various functions in the village. The most outgoing of the octet was a small, green-eyed girl with high cheekbones and a neat, though slightly twisted nose, that looked as if it hadn't been reset properly following an accident: Giselle Cornthwaite by name, and the rider of a sleek grey called Puzzle. Two or three times as they changed she glanced across at Ros and smiled, but apart from murmuring 'Good luck' to each other as they filed out of the tent, heading for the parade ring, they didn't converse.

Saskia Sound, she was pleased to discover, had a kind eye and appeared relaxed. 'Good as gold, she is today,' murmured Hazel, the stable lass in charge of her. Ros was thankful to hear it and it seemed to her that the chestnut mare was a very placid individual who would be no trouble to ride in a race. But experience with a number of highly-strung horses had taught her that appearances like that were all too often deceptive.

'Well, you're lovely, aren't you?' she said, rubbing Saskia's nose with her knuckles.

'Yeah, I'm sure you're in for a good ride,' agreed Nigel Trent. 'Just keep her up to the mark on the first circuit and then win if you can. But come home safe, whatever you do. OK?'

'OK, sir,' Ros replied formally now that she was officially taking over the owner's horse. She'd expected him to be much more demanding, full of instructions to do this and avoid that and desperate for the mare to win. He was none of those things and that attitude was comforting to her. Best of all, he appeared genuinely concerned for her safety above everything else.

As soon as she was in the saddle everything felt right: and her hopes rose higher than the fences she so soon would face. Saskia Sound had a lovely, swinging gait and seemed to know exactly what was expected of her (which, as Ros knew from experience, wasn't always the case, even with horses which raced regularly: they seemed to think that what they were being asked to do today was totally different from what they did yesterday – or perhaps, on second thoughts, they simply didn't think at all). She carefully tested the steering on the canter to the start and, once again, Saskia made all the right responses.

The mare looked about her a little but that was natural enough; if she exercised on this grassland she wouldn't be used to seeing so many people and vehicles about. Cars, some that must have cost more than many a four-bedroom house, others that appeared to have been rescued from the scrapyard at the last minute, were dotted all over the circuit as their drivers and passengers sought a private grandstand view of the proceedings.

The start was predictably ragged. With more than two miles to race and more than a dozen fences to jump, no one seemed to think that the few yards given away at the outset mattered very much; and, what's more, no one was anxious to set the pace. Just before the off Ros had learned from Phil Swift that although Time Trial was a warm favourite, there'd been several loud whispers for a young horse called Pascal who'd travelled from a distant county. And it was Pascal, an eager dark bay, who forged ahead the moment his rider, Fiona, eased the restraints. He took the first fence literally in his stride, popping over it as if it were no higher than a training hurdle.

Saskia Sound jumped the obstacle in second place. Ros, too, saw no point in holding her mount back when she was so keen to race. Nigel Trent had told her to make her own decisions about how to run the race and it seemed that Saskia was enjoying herself: and a horse that was happy in

83

its work would always do its best when you asked it for a real effort. She viewed the fence a trifle cautiously but jumped it fluently enough and was smoothly into her stride again on landing.

'Phe-ew!' Ros expelled a long breath which she hadn't realized she was holding. Now the first critical moment of their partnership was over: they'd survived it intact. More, it had given Ros an injection of confidence at their prospects. She reached down to fondle Saskia's left ear – and the next instant almost found herself on the ground! For the mare's reaction to that friendly touch was to swerve sharply to the left before correcting her course. Quite plainly, she didn't like to have her ear touched while running.

'Sorry, girl!' Ros called, tentatively giving the mare a pat down the neck and hoping that wouldn't alarm her, too. She just wished Hazel had confided that dislike to her when handing over the horse; but, of course, it was entirely possible that Hazel herself wasn't aware of all Saskia's little foibles. Sometimes horses themselves displayed quite different reactions under what were almost identical circumstances.

That abrupt swerve hadn't, as it turned out, made any difference to the running order. Saskia was still in second place, about three lengths adrift of Pascal, with the grey Puzzle and Time Trial sharing third place a further two lengths behind. The first fence was so innocuous that everyone jumped it comfortably. The muddier stretches of the track, where horses had come to grief in earlier races, lay well ahead of them. The pace was undemanding and no one was yet under any pressure. For Ros, riding an unknown quantity, this was the ideal situation.

At the third fence, however, things changed quite quickly. Pascal unaccountably made a hash of it, clouting it very hard and almost catapulting his rider out of the saddle; and his momentum was gone, at least temporarily. Amanda, on Time Trial, decided simultaneously that this was the moment to exert herself and, slapping her whip fairly lightly down his neck, she urged the favourite to close up. Puzzle, who'd been enjoying Time Trial's company, wasn't at all pleased by this departure and decided to follow suit; but Giselle wasn't having that and yanked him back with rare force. Giselle was a good deal stronger and tougher than she looked.

Saskia Sound was still moving serenely and Ros was beginning to enjoy herself; she even had time to wonder why Saskia wasn't better thought of by Nigel and some of his friends. So, in spite of her pleasure in the ride so far, Ros remained wary, ready to deal with whatever emergency might arise: for, clearly, no one expected her to have a trouble-free round and the mare was not one of the market leaders. Perhaps that drastic reaction to having her ear touched was the real indication of Saskia's suspect temperament.

Pascal didn't allow his near-disaster at the third fence to bother him for long and with Time Trial now ranging alongside he began to stretch out again. He liked to dictate his own pace. Fiona was one of the most experienced riders in the field and she was well aware that it was best, for the time being, to let Pascal run his own race in his own way. He'd shown in the past that he learned from his mistakes, rarely repeating them in the same race or the next. The presence of Time Trial was really what he needed to make him concentrate on his work. So for the best part of a mile the joint leaders jumped together, jumped fast and jumped accurately. For the spectators, wherever they were positioned around the circuit, it was an exhilarating spectacle and there was often spontaneous applause for horses and riders from those standing by the fences being jumped.

Ros, who had approached that dangerous fifth fence with caution but negotiated it without a semblance of difficulty, now faced a problem in tactics as the leaders drew steadily further and further ahead: should she kick-on and go in pursuit or be patient and wait for the pacesetters to lose some of their momentum and slow down, as surely they would? It was a dilemma she'd experienced in the past but on other occasions she'd had a good knowledge of the horse she was riding. Not so with Saskia. Still, it would be foolish to lay too far back, so leaving her mount with perhaps too much to do in the closing stages. She had no idea whether Saskia possessed finishing speed, that prerequisite of most successful racehorses.

So, without demanding too much too soon, she encouraged the chestnut with no more than a touch of her heels and the movement of her hands. Saskia quickened nicely and Ros felt a surge of joy in her veins: this was just the sort of response she would hope for from a thoroughbred on the Downs above Tildown House. Of course, a point-to-pointer could never compare in performance with a racehorse of Mantola's calibre; but that quickening, the spontaneity of it, was a sure sign of ability.

Ros knew now that, whatever else happened in the remaining minutes, this wasn't going to be a two-horse race between that exuberant bay, Pascal, and Amanda Glossup's favourite. In due course, Saskia would be challenging them. Meanwhile, she glanced over her shoulder to check on the whereabouts of Puzzle. He, still fighting for his head, was at least three lengths behind them; so far there'd been only one faller and the rest of the field was well strung out.

In spite of the increased pace Saskia took the next two obstacles with the same economy of action and no loss of momentum on touching down. Suddenly the leaders were right in Ros's sights again.

'Come on, girl, we can win this, we can!' she called out ecstatically. At that point they were on the side of the course furthest from the makeshift grandstands and thus, because of a natural dip in the ground, out of sight of most spectators and officials. In fact, there was only one person who

86

heard Ros's excited remark. And that was Giselle Corn-thwaite who had stealthily closed the gap between them since jumping the previous obstacle. She made her decisive move just as Ros was gathering Saskia for the next fence. Out of the corner of her right eye Ros glimpsed the looming figure of the grey horse and was taken by surprise. The grey seemed to be about to lean in on her.

'Hey, give me some room!' she was yelling when, to her horror, she felt her right boot being hooked out of the stirrup and pressure exerted under the instep. It took some moments for her to realize that Giselle was deliberately trying to tip her out of the saddle!

The attempt had been carried out so skilfully that the horses hadn't even bumped. Saskia, still flowing sweetly towards the fence, was unaffected by the loose iron and, launching herself at the barrier, cleared it without touching so much as a single twig.

Ros, only momentarily unnerved, struggled to locate the swinging stirrup and put her toe into it. Giselle and Puzzle had once again dropped back a little and were now about two lengths behind Saskia. There was really no time for Ros to dwell on that astonishing incident. She had to put it out of her mind and concentrate on riding to win. Often enough in the hurly-burly of a point-to-point she had suffered some interference at a fence from a horse out of control or through the sheer carelessness of an incompetent rider. You learned to accept that and get on with riding your horse to the best of your ability. At least you were still in the saddle and not painfully stretched out or crumpled up on the deck.

In any case, that wasn't the only surprise development. At the very next fence, another open ditch, Pascal took off much too soon and paid the inevitable penalty; hitting the obstacle really hard, he tilted on his nose and catapulted Fiona into the ground on the landing side of the fence. Time Trial, who'd been jumping upsides the bay, went over in style and his rider, hearing the carnage on her near side, sensed that the way to the post was now clear. Before the next fence, the penultimate one, Amanda risked a glance over her shoulder to see what the opposition were up to; but she was confident that, barring a fall, the Ladies' Open Race (and quite handsome silver trophy) were hers. She could afford to smile at Fiona's misfortune because Pascal was the only horse she'd feared could snatch the prize from her.

That calamity for Fiona acted as a spur to Ros. Now there was only one opponent between her and victory. True, Time Trial was well ahead but Ros had still not asked her mount for any real effort. Saskia, she felt sure, had plenty of power in reserve for she had been running so easily without displaying any sign at all of fatigue. If Time Trial weakened under pressure, or was lacking in finishing speed, then the next two or three minutes would find that out.

Giselle, however, had her own ideas about the outcome of the race. The failure of her attempt to unseat one rival she regarded merely as an insignificant setback. Next time she would succeed in her objective. Her experience of some years of riding in point-to-points told her that Saskia Sound really was going very well and might be about to recapture the sort of form she'd displayed in her heyday. If she, Giselle, was to triumph then Saskia had to be stopped, and stopped quickly. One plan had failed; but another sprang to mind almost immediately. Giselle was nothing if not resourceful; those cool green eyes reflected a cool, sharp brain. Now she set about igniting Puzzle for her next move and then the race to the finishing post.

In her anxiety to catch Time Trial Ros didn't take her usual care when approaching that penultimate fence; by now she'd begun to assume that Saskia would put herself right for it without any assistance. But the mare was beginning to tire. She'd run and jumped almost immaculately and enjoyed herself; yet it was a long time since she'd been racing. Lack of peak condition was starting to tell. To anyone who'd ridden her before, that might have been evident at the previous fence when she had veered slightly off line just before taking off; but Ros, without that personal knowledge of her and with other things on her mind, hadn't seen any significance in her manoeuvre. Now, however, Saskia didn't rise quite high enough; her belly brushed through the birch and she landed awkwardly. Ros, marginally jolted by the experience, moved quickly to pick her mount up and resume their challenge to the leader. No real damage had been done to their chances, she was sure.

But now Puzzle was coming alongside again and Ros turned her head instinctively to see what threat was being posed this time. Behind her goggles Giselle's eyes were calm as ever but her voice managed to blend compassion with matter-of-factness as she called out,

'Pull up if you want to save your horse! She nearly cut her leg off at that fence!'

Automatically Ros dropped her hands. Any possibility of a horse being injured brought out an immediate reaction in her: it was one of the reasons why Angela Sagaro had such faith in her, more faith than ever Ros herself imagined. She had a natural empathy with horses that encompassed deep concern for their well-being. It was only when Puzzle and Giselle swept past them and Saskia slowed almost to a canter that it occurred to Ros that once again Giselle was determined to stop them winning.

She had been preparing to dismount but now, instead, she glanced down, first at Saskia's off-hind leg, then at the near-hind leg. Everything looked perfectly normal. There wasn't a sign of blood or damaged skin. So far as she could tell there wasn't even a scratch anywhere. If Saskia Sound had really been hurt in any way then it certainly didn't show. She hadn't flinched and her action hadn't changed. She had simply slowed down and was now moving at almost walking pace.

'Come on, girl, come on!' Ros yelled to rouse her. She

didn't like to use a whip, ever, but there was a time for everything: and this was the time for a sharp crack behind the saddle. It was desperately unfair on the mare because she hadn't done anything to deserve such treatment. Ros didn't know how her mount would react; but Saskia's temperament was flawless. She simply did as she was bid and picked up speed in spite of her tiredness.

Puzzle was still in hot pursuit of the leader: and seemed to have every chance of catching him. Time Trial, too, was slowing down and, at the final fence, faltered quite badly: which gave the redoubtable, remorseless Giselle further encouragement. The one certainty now was that the race lay between Puzzle and Time Trial and the crowd, sensing an all-out battle to the line, was beginning to cheer vociferously.

Ros was thinking how her riding might be viewed from the stands. No one would have any idea that Giselle had told her to pull up to save her horse from further injury; it would simply look as though she'd decided to stop racing – and then changed her mind. Quite possibly people would even imagine she was deliberately trying to make sure she *didn't* win the race! If the officials took that view then she'd be in real trouble. Even if they didn't, Nigel Trent would have reason to be furious with her for riding such an ill-judged race.

She was determined to finish in the first three; at least that would be some achievement after all the mishaps in the past few minutes. Although Saskia Sound had rallied and was running on quite well, Ros didn't want to give her a hard race. She might be justified, in racing terms, in giving her a few more whacks with the whip but that wouldn't bring victory or even a close finish for a place. Saskia would surely resent such treatment and might refuse to co-operate. Ros took a quick look over her shoulder and saw that her nearest pursuer was within a couple of lengths. If that horse, Sombrero by name, possessed stamina, then in all likelihood Saskia wouldn't collect third place. Which would be a poor reward for Nigel Trent's – and Phil Swift's – confidence in their rider.

The last fence, which Time Trial had struggled over, now loomed up. Ros collected her horse with great care and directed her towards the very centre of the fence and the firmest ground on the landing side. 'You can do it, Saskia, you can do it!' she urged. And Saskia did, sailing over almost as if it were the first obstacle instead of the last. Ros expelled a breath of relief. She was positive now that they would finish third. It was just possible they might even snatch second place because Time Trial appeared to be labouring and Puzzle looked the likely winner.

Gradually, metre by metre, Puzzle, under the strongest driving from Giselle, closed on Time Trial. But, as the most observant and knowledgeable of the spectators had noted, Amanda was still riding the favourite with hands and heels. Not once had Time Trial been shown the whip.

With no more than fifty metres to go the grey, sweating profusely, drew level with the leader and the roar from the crowd was loud and sustained. Plenty of money was riding on Giselle's horse and the punters were about to count their winnings. But Amanda Glossup knew exactly what she was doing: her partnership with Time Trial stretched back a long time and, in races, it was usually victorious. Now, with the winning post practically within reach, she gave her horse a single hard slap down the neck. And Time Trial surged ahead again to win practically by a length. The favourite's backers cheered with as much relief as delight.

Ros was as thankful as any of Amanda's supporters that Giselle hadn't won. As soon as she passed the winning post in third place, a comfortable couple of lengths in front of Sombrero, she made a point of riding up to Amanda to shake hands; she ignored Giselle, for the moment.

'Well, now, that wasn't too bad at all, was it?' remarked

Nigel Trent, raising his hat to her as she began to unsaddle Saskia. He managed to look quite pleased.

'I'm terribly sorry, Mr Trent,' Ros said. The disappointment in her voice was unmistakable. 'I'm sure we could have won – or nearly, anyway – if I hadn't stopped riding after the second last.'

He gave her an appraising look. 'Well, I don't know about that, young lady. I think the old girl did pretty well after being off the track for a while. But what went wrong, anyway?'

Ros had decided that there was nothing at all to be gained by telling the truth. In all likelihood it would just sound like an excuse or, at least, sour grapes. She guessed that all people deeply involved in racing knew that dirty tricks were part of the game when money was at stake. Unless they were too blatant to be ignored, they were considered to be no more than one of the hazards of the sport.

'I thought Saskia had hurt herself as we brushed through that fence, damaged a leg, cut a tendon, something like that,' Ros said as convincingly as she could manage. 'But I couldn't see or feel anything after a few strides and she seemed as sound as a bell. So, well, I had to wake her up a bit then. But it was too late. Sorry, Mr Trent.'

He shook his head. 'Don't worry about it, Rosalind. You did a good job. I was quite impressed by your horsemanship. Honestly, I didn't expect her to win even if Phil Swift did! But I warned him not to bet too heavily. Still, I expect he can afford it. No, a place is good enough for me.' He paused a moment, gave her a straight look and added: 'Next time you ride her I think you'll do even better. Is that a deal?'

'Oh yes,' she replied, smiling eagerly, 'it's a deal all right! I'll really look forward to another ride on Saskia.'

She wasn't smiling a few minutes later when she came face to face with Giselle Cornthwaite in the ladies' changing-room. She felt like hitting her, even scratching those cool, impersonal, treacherous green eyes, but instead she just said what was in her mind.

'You rotten bitch! You *knew* there was nothing wrong with my horse. You just wanted to stop us having a chance of winning.'

Giselle's gaze didn't waver. 'Nothing of the sort. When you made a hash of that fence I thought I saw blood flying. Must have been sweat. Didn't want your horse to suffer unduly.'

'Well, I'm thankful you lost! And I'll tell you this, Miss Dirty Tricks. You ever cross my path again and I'll gallop all over you, bury you for good. That's not a warning. It's a promise.'

After that there was nothing more anyone could say. Their conversation had taken place at one end of the changing-room, out of earshot of the other girls, and now Ros strode to the opposite corner of the room and sank down beside her pile of clothes. In spite of Nigel Trent's generous reaction and promise of another ride she was feeling distinctly hard done by and fed up. She wished that Lydia were there so that she could tell her of her feelings; whatever faults Lydia might have, she was an excellent and sympathetic listener.

'I feel I've been kicked in the teeth by fate so many times lately,' she would have said. 'So I'm going to kick back when I get the chance, just like any normal horse would do if it had been badly treated. It's the only thing you can do, isn't it?'

Because she was so absorbed by her own thoughts and internal conversation it was some time before she became aware of what the two girls sitting next to her were talking about. One of them, she recognized, was the rider of the horse that had fallen quite early in the race; the other was the girl who had finished last on a roan gelding that hadn't the speed to overtake donkeys on the sand at the seaside.

'He's so useless I've got to get rid of him, if anybody else is stupid enough to take him off my hands,' the second girl was saying so fiercely it was plain she meant it. 'I can't stand another ride like today's. It's – it's humiliating!'

'Well, there is that auction at Rattlestone, up on the ridge,' her friend remarked. 'My uncle once sold one of his old shire horses up there, half-crippled it was, but it fetched a decent price.

'The weirdest people turn up to buy and sell, Uncle told us. But it's all supposed to be a bit secretive in case, well, there's any criminals involved. Must be, from what I heard. So if you're really desperate, Karen, you could always try to flog your poor old nag up there. You just don't have to think too much about what could happen afterwards!'

'I might *just*!' Karen said with theatrical emphasis. 'When's the next auction, do you know, Sallie?'

'Well, if you really mean it, you could be in luck because I believe there's one next Wednesday,' Sallie told her in a lowered, almost conspiratorial tone. 'But it's late at night for obvious reasons. If you do go, you'd better take someone with you as a minder! Up there you'll come across some types you wouldn't want to meet in a main street in the middle of the day, let alone in the middle of the moors on a dark night!'

'Oh, well, perhaps I'll think about it,' Karen said, her resolution suddenly weakening. 'I mean, I wouldn't want anything *really* terrible to happen to Lampeter just because he's so slow and useless. Though, well, it would be nice to get hold of some decent money for him, I suppose. Yes, I'll think about it, Sallie . . .'

Ros, who hadn't said a word to either of the girls or even glanced in their direction while eavesdropping on their conversation, now knew with complete certainty where she would be next Wednesday night.

Eight

There was mist and chill in the air and an eerie sense of isolation from the rest of the world. It was, Ros had no doubt, no doubt at all, a night for dark deeds. But she was prepared to endure any situation, however dangerous, if she could be reunited with Mantola. What her chances were of that she had no way of calculating but she supposed an honest bookie would put them at a thousand-to-one at least. Yet her instincts, coupled with the image that Agatha Elliott had forseen of a raised hammer, had propelled her towards Rattlestone Moor. It was her belief that she was destined to see her horse again and she would have been perfectly willing to face odds of a million-to-one.

Her inquiries about the auction had necessarily been discreet. Angela Sagaro claimed that she knew nothing about it, yet within an hour of hearing Ros's question she was suggesting that Mrs Leatherbarrow, the lady who single-handedly ran a flourishing agricultural feeds business and the owner of a horse Ros had ridden in point-to-points, might have some information. When Ros telephoned her she learned that the auctions took place in a dilapidated barn on the site of a former farmstead on the end of the Ridge, the area known as Rattlestone Moor. In spite of the secrecy which was supposed to surround the event, plenty of people actually knew about it: they had to because the horses for sale came from a variety of sources.

'But if you're thinking of attending you'd better have a

good excuse for being there,' Mrs Leatherbarrow advised. 'The men who run it post guards at strategic points on every conceivable approach to the Big Barn. Unless you can convince them you've a right to be there they'll not let you past them. So be warned, my dear, be warned. Best keep away altogether if you want my best advice.'

Nothing at all would have kept Ros away from the chance of finding Mantola. Her planning was meticulous. She'd take her bike as far as the top of the Downs and conceal it there in the bushes with Mantola's saddle and tack; the rest of the way she would walk because her fervent hope was that she would be riding back on Mantola. She couldn't imagine she'd have enough money even to put down a deposit on his purchase: and, anyway, it was hardly likely the sellers would be interested in a part-payment system! None the less she took what she could raise from her bank and building society accounts. It had occurred to her that she might have to bribe somebody to help her in some way. Her other precaution was to carry a bag of pepper. She had her fingers crossed that she wouldn't need to use it.

Now, just ahead of her, she could make out a yellowish glow, a flare-like light that was extinguished almost in the same moment she detected it. Ros paused, sure now that she was close to the abandoned farmstead for, moments earlier, she had clambered over a shattered, low stone wall, probably the original boundary wall of the property. Silence surrounded her, a silence that was beginning to be unnerving. She took a step forward – and someone grabbed her arm above the elbow.

Ros screamed. She couldn't help it. But even to herself it sounded like a squeak.

'Who are you?' a man's voice demanded. She couldn't believe that anyone could have got so close to her without her being aware of it. His breath was on her ear.

'My name's Karen,' she gasped, trying to prise his fingers

from her arm. 'Karen Simpson.' Where that name had materialized from she had no idea.

'What d'you want then?' His voice was strong but not rough. He didn't sound like a villain.

'A horse, of course.' Because of the rhyme she even managed to laugh, though it wasn't with amusement. 'Look, I've got money. I'm ready to pay good money.'

She fished the roll of banknotes out of her anorak pocket and her captor shone a torch. She'd gambled. He could so easily have snatched the money from her and vanished. She might not have dared to follow him. But he didn't. He grunted and switched the torch off. She'd gambled – and won.

'Go to the entrance on the left, tell Red One that Yellow One has passed you. Got that, kid?'

'Yes,' she answered, and was released. When she walked away she expelled a breath she hadn't known she was holding. The bulk of the building loomed up within a few strides. Even when talking to Yellow One she had had no idea that she was so close to the Big Barn. Now, because she saw no other people approaching it, she assumed she was too early and that no one else would be there, although it was already nearly midnight.

The door was framed by a dim light because it no longer fitted properly, only adequately. It swung inwards the moment she put her fingers to it and the scene she came upon astounded her. Candles high on poles supplemented the illumination provided by a dozen or more spotlamps and lanterns. And all that temporary light surrounded a ring like a cockpit. Ros thought first of a cathedral during Mass; and then of a theatre-in-the-round production that was proceeding in spite of a local power failure. The audience was already present, crowded everywhere around the elliptical circle except for one segment where it was joined by a broad path. Along that path a horse was being led from a still darker region at the back of the barn.

97

Somewhere beyond that, Ros supposed, lay the stalls (if such refinements existed in this place) or lines where the horses to be sold were kept waiting.

Once again Ros was taken unawares as an arm thumped across her chest. She recoiled but managed to blurt out: 'Yellow One passed me.'

There was no word in response but the arm was withdrawn. Her fingers, deep in one of her side pockets, thankfully released the bag of pepper they'd been grasping. She took a few steps towards the arena, pushing between groups of men intent on their talk and gestures and opinions. There was scarcely another female to be seen. The men were of every age and, Ros guessed, from many backgrounds: farmers, dealers in junk as well as horseflesh, garagemen and shopkeepers, bookmakers and dole men by the dozen. She had decided to make her way to the back of the barn because there she might be able to inspect the horses still to be sold. If, among them, she found Mantola . . . what then? She had a plan but hardly dared believe it would work.

A couple of metres from the back wall she met an impasse, a band of bidders who weren't disposed to let her through when a sale was about to take place. So, rather than cause a scene which could lead to her summary eviction, she turned to watch. And saw the auctioneer's hammer rise to call for silence – and saw the flickering candlelight all around the cockpit – and saw again the crystal ball in Agatha Elliott's house when Mrs Elliott had told her of just such a scene. Her heart began to beat with increased urgency and anticipation. She would watch this sale, see how it was done and what happened to the horse when it was sold; and then she'd try again to make her way to wherever the rest of the horses were being kept.

Lot Whatever-its-number was led in on a short rope, led in at a fast trot so that the customers could judge its paces, led in sullenly, unhappily, miserably even. Ros was

98

shocked by its shaggy appearance: it must have been weeks, if not months, since it had felt a brush or clippers. Why on earth did they display it in that way? Surely the idea of an auction was to present the object for sale in the very best light to fetch the very best price?

That didn't appear to be the policy here. Perhaps the theory was that buyers knew exactly what they wanted, what everything was really worth, and so they couldn't be conned into paying above the odds. If the horse had been stolen then it hardly mattered, in one way, what price it made: because just about every penny paid over would be profit for the vendor.

Ros pressed forward for a better view of the horse. It wasn't at all the kind she was used to but, as a young girl in love with every kind of horse, she'd studied different breeds and could remember many of them. This, she was certain, was a Connemara, an odd colouring, a darkly spotted grey with black socks (or was that simply encrusted dirt?), a filthy long mane and the saddest eyes Ros had ever seen. Its handler kept jerking the horse's head up and down, up and down, as the auctioneer in a fairly monotonous tone extolled the animal's apparently endless virtues: tough, hard-working, good jumper ('Leap a decent fence without so much as looking at it,' was the totally improbable claim), needing the minimum of care. 'So now, gentlemen, what will ye offer me for this very decent animal?' Decent was clearly one of his favourite words: and the paradox was not lost on Ros.

She studied the horse's configuration, the faintly sloping hindquarters, the shortish sturdy legs, the once quite handsome head. It was, she was now confident, a Connemara, so what on earth was it doing here, in southern England? What sort of life had it led in recent years to finish up at an illicit auction in a candlelit barn at midnight? Why was it being sold at all instead of being given a comfortable retirement in a favourite paddock? Did its owner so desperately need the few pounds it could be sold for? Did the owner even *know* the horse was up for sale here?

The bidding for the pony was slow, lethargic really, as though its appearance had put most prospective buyers off. Ros couldn't spot the bids that were being made until a man beside her knocked her shoulder as his arm went up: but it really was just one finger he was raising. She glanced up at him but his expression gave nothing away and when the bidding became brisker and he dropped out he was still emotionless. Towards the end there was a flurry of bids before, after a protracted interval, the winning one. Jerking his rope yet more fiercely the handler practically dragged the Connemara from the arena to whatever fate lay in store for him. The final price surprised Ros: she hadn't expected such a lot of money to be paid for a pony with what was surely an uncertain working future. Disappointingly, she couldn't tell who had bought him.

The next lot, as the auctioneer intoned, was a complete contrast: a well-groomed, handsome stallion, a dark chestnut with a curious zig-zaggy blaze and unmistakable Arab blood in his veins. The auctioneer kept making the point that this was a stallion and with a long career at stud ahead of him and progeny that could fetch thousands. He was only being allowed to leave his present stable because of over-crowding, a remark that drew a number of disbelieving jeers from the crowd. The auctioneer peered over his half-spectacles as if trying to identify such ill-mannered people; he even waved his gavel in a mildly disapproving way. 'Walk on again, walk on,' he instructed the handler who duly took the horse round the tight circuit so that his action could be properly admired.

Ros expected that he would be in demand – she would have loved to bid for him herself – and she was right. Even the first bid of all was pitched at a high level, perhaps in the hope that other prospective buyers would be instantly discouraged, and this time Ros was able to detect some of the nods and raised eyebrows and vertical fingers that constituted offers for the horse.

Yet, once again, there was a long pause after the price had reached a certain plateau before the second of two more emphatic bids proved to be the conclusive one. So the horse with the blood of Arabian lines in its veins disappeared from view and the buzz of talk from bidders and watchers suddenly grew louder. There was a little shifting, too, in the crowd and Ros decided this might be the best moment to make a determined move towards the rear of the barn to see the horses due to appear centre stage shortly.

But then, as she caught a glimpse of the horse being led towards the sale ring, she stopped dead.

There was no mistaking that arrogant toss of the head, that swinging stride even in such confined surroundings, that challenging stare as he came to a halt in front of the auctioneer. The halter the handler was holding was longer than those used for previous 'lots' while the handler himself displayed the sort of care for his charge that had been noticeably absent among the other men. This man was just as alert as the others had been but he was younger and better dressed. For Ros, however, only the horse mattered.

'Oh, Mantola, Mantola!' she murmured fervently. 'I've found you, found you at last.'

Since reaching Rattlestone Moor she had never doubted that she would find him. Her faith in Agatha Elliott's vision was now vindicated. She didn't even wonder how it was possible for Mrs Elliott to visualize that candlelight and the rise and fall of an auctioneer's hammer. She simply accepted that, somehow, it was ordained, that she and Mantola were destined to be reunited in this crumbling and crammed barn on the edge of the moors. Her faith in the plan she had devised to free them both from this awful place was less strong but it couldn't be changed now.

'Well, gentlemen, this could be the one ye've all been waiting for,' exclaimed the auctioneer, persistent in his refusal to acknowledge that there were *some* women in his audience, though perhaps he was the only one aware that none of them was bidding.

Momentarily, both observers and prospective purchasers had fallen silent as they studied the potential of the horse in the ring. Did they see him as a likely winner at some foreign race meeting or even triumphant, under another name and subtly changed in appearance, at a point-to-point meeting in a remote corner of England? Ros didn't dare contemplate other possibilities for his future if she failed to take him back to his rightful home. Now, urgently, she needed too make her way through the press of bodies to reach the place where the horses changed hands.

Suddenly, she was face to face with Tony Vasson. The shock was so great she simply stared at him, feeling her eyes widen and her heart begin to thump painfully again. He recovered the quicker, a wolfish grin spreading across his narrow face.

'Come to find me, have you, Miss Hayward? Or is it Ros now we're off-duty?' he asked.

'I – I –' she started. But she really didn't know what to say. She wished he hadn't used her name like that because anyone might have picked it up; and anonymity was vital to her if her plan was to succeed. Inevitably, he looked pleased with her bewilderment.

'Are you here to buy a horse?' she managed to inquire. She might have guessed he would be here because men like Tony Vasson had always had a place on the crooked fringe of racing.

'Might do, might do,' he murmured. 'Might do anything at all I fancy.' He barely paused: 'And I think I fancy you, Miss Ros.'

His hand suddenly snaked under her anorak. She tried to pull herself free but in such a crush of people she had no room to manoeuvre. 'No, not now, not now!' she said urgently, hoping he would desist for what might sound to him like a promise.

But she saw that his jaw was working from side to side, a sure sign that something was bothering him. 'You don't like me, do you, you and that Miss Kent?' he said; it was more a statement than a question.

Ros had to deny it. 'Yes we do! You're, er, great on the gallops.'

His grin returned. 'I'm great in other ways, too.' His hand in her anorak was now beginning to explore in earnest. 'We could have a great time together after all the buying and selling's over. Just – '

'NO!' Her foot crashed down on his instep and the pain made him release his hold on her. She dived away from him.

Ros suffered abuse and the sharp jabs of elbows as she determinedly pushed through the crowd. By now the auction for Mantola had started and bids were being signalled briskly; but Ros had no idea at all where they were coming from or whether she was even interrupting any.

'You can't get through this way – get lost!' an overweight man in a dirty sheepskin spat at her. Ros simply darted round him, ducking her body through the narrowest gap and then apologizing quickly for stepping heavily on someone's foot, accidentally this time. She received another jab in the ribs but there was no point in complaining. All that mattered was that she escaped from Tony Vasson and got to her objective, got there before Mantola was sold and dismissed from the arena so that another transaction could take place. Once again the noise level had fallen dramatically as if the audience knew that the climax of the play had arrived. And, indeed, only two bidders now remained in the contest to secure Mantola. The final bid would signal the end of another tense drama.

Ros didn't hear it. Almost breathless from her struggles and the buffetings she'd received she reached the rear wall and the gap through which the horses were being brought in from a flagged yard. At last she could pause and try to get her bearings before making her next move – the most crucial move in the entire plan.

The last bid was made with no more than the nod of a bearded face beneath a black hat: and when the man's solitary opponent shook his own head so positively that his earrings danced the auctioneer knocked Mantola down at a price that brought a smattering of applause from the onlookers. Then, as curtly as ever, he indicated to the young handler that the horse could be taken away.

Mantola came swinging up the narrow corridor between the lines of men who believed themselves adept at judging horseflesh and what it would fetch, per race or per kilogram or perhaps through progeny. The boy leading him was surprisingly rosy-cheeked, a girlish colouring that didn't tone with his broad black moustache; he looked relieved, probably because his duties were almost over, undoubtedly because he would pick up a bonus related to the sale price. The horse had been really no trouble at all, though the boy thought he did rather fancy himself, the cocky type, the sort who looked good in the parade ring but never won when *he* had backed them. Still, this pay was a hell of a lot better than just landing a winning bet, especially considering the sort of stake he could afford to put on at a betting shop.

Ros had edged out of the barn and into the yard where the clatter of pawing hooves on the flags drowned all noise from the selling area. She'd feared that some sentry or look-out would ask what she was up to but no one did. By now it had been assumed that because the auction had been going on for some time there would be no trouble from within; the only guards were those posted in a loosely-linked ring on a radius of more than two hundred metres from the centre of the barn. A lorry was lurching away down a rough track, taking the Connemara to its new home even further from Ireland than its previous one. Men were busy with harness and shovel, brush and bridle, and no one had any time for Ros. In this light, although improving now as cloud cleared and the moon brightened, she was not noticeable either for her youthfulness or for her physical attractions. Neither could anyone see how desperately nervous she was.

The boy was slowing down, naturally enough, as he emerged from the exit door and Mantola, having received no word or signal to do likewise, bumped him in the back, knocking him off-balance. That was the touch of luck Ros had been praying for. As the boy, recovering, turned to swear at the culprit, Ros stepped smartly forward.

'Here,' she said, taking the halter with one hand and slapping a chinking bag of money into the boy's palm with the other hand, 'this is for you. From my boss, this one's new owner.'

For a moment or two that was vitally in Ros's favour, the boy didn't react. He hadn't known quite what to expect, or who to expect, when he led the horse from the sale ring. All he had guessed was that someone would come to take the horse off him. The money bag was a splendid surprise and his fingers tightened round it as he instinctively released the halter.

Mantola's ears shot forward as he recognized Ros's voice. He took a step towards her.

'Hey Manty, hold on!' she said softly, slapping his neck and then putting her arm across his back. The spring off her left foot was all she'd hoped for; and so, without any time lost, she was on his bare back and with her knees urging him forward, down the yard, between the scatterings of horses and grooms and hangers-on. With only a head collar to steer by, she felt vulnerable already; but she'd ridden Mantola without proper harness many times and that experience was now invaluable.

Of course, it was the girl's leap on to the horse's back that alerted the boy to the fact that something was wrong. If she'd continued to lead him away he might not have realized that anything was wrong until the new owners came to collect the horse. As luck had it, he hadn't heard Ros call the horse by its name – he'd simply been aware that she spoke to it as anyone taking charge of a horse would do to establish command. He wanted to count his bonus before anything else and that was why he hesitated: fatally, as it turned out, for his chances of escaping censure for his incompetence. But the speed with which the girl was taking the horse away was suspicious . . .

'Hey, just a minute,' he yelled, though not very authoritatively. One or two of the other grooms glanced up, surprised that anyone should make unnecessary noise at such a time; and the nearest horse backed away from its handler. But no one else took any notice.

Ros rode on. Her major concern, now, was the man sure to be guarding the track along which the horseboxes were travelling: the track she would have to use before she could head away across the open moorland. But his worries would centre on anyone coming from the opposite direction to see what was happening in the old barn; he wouldn't expect trouble from those departing with the horses they'd acquired in the sale ring. On the other hand, he probably wouldn't expect anyone to *ride* a horse away, either. So . . . she felt in her pocket and took out the bag of pepper. It was the best weapon she'd been able to think of and it would certainly immobilize an opponent if her aim was good.

Ahead of her the trundling horsebox of the new owner of the Connemara pony was slowing to a halt. The driver wanted a word with the guard at the end of the track. He wasn't absolutely sure of the right direction to take at the crossroads just this side of the village. If he could save a few miles on another route, well, he'd be home faster than he'd promised . . .

Suddenly it occurred to Ros what to do. Instead of giving the van and the sentry a wide berth she asked Mantola to quicken so that she could pass them both as close as possible while the box was stationary.

'Night then!' she called in as deep a voice as possible, waving an arm in salute. Both driver and guard paused in their conversation; but only for a moment. Then, each believing that the passing horseman was, almost literally, a passing acquaintance, they each returned a casual wave. After all, those up to no good didn't call out friendly greetings. It was those with something to hide who tried to keep out of sight while creeping past you.

The driver learned what he wanted to know and then, revving up and laboriously engaging gear, he chugged away across Rattlestone Moor. Ros aimed Mantola in the opposite direction. Her ambition was to get as far away from the barn as possible in the shortest time. But she daren't go too fast because of all the hazards underfoot. The moorland terrain was uneven, to say the least; there were dips and boggy patches and dreadful pot-holes, any one of which could cause a disaster. If Mantola stumbled and threw her off and then took fright for some reason she might never catch up with him again. So, even though she was worried about possible pursuers, they had to move cautiously.

The light from the moon was better than she'd feared: but, again, that had its disadvantages because it would be just as helpful to anyone trying to find them. So far she had heard no sounds of pursuit. Yet by now the boy would have relayed the news to his employers (or whoever they were) that the horse had been stolen: an irony they would definitely not appreciate! They would be the ones who would want to give chase to recover 'their' property. Ros supposed that the person who'd bought Mantola wouldn't have paid over his money before the news reached him that his horse was missing. So, if he hadn't parted with the money, he wouldn't suffer any actual loss, only, presumably, disappointment that he wasn't getting what he wanted. But, as the sale wasn't over yet, there was still a chance that he could pick up another horse that took his fancy.

Would the thieves give chase? Ros decided that, on balance, they probably would. After all, they were in danger of losing a valuable property, one they'd already managed to 'sell' for a lot of money: money they wouldn't get unless they retrieved the horse. They would also look pretty foolish, to put it mildly, if they had to admit that they couldn't protect their own property. Anyone who'd been outwitted in the way they had been would be furious, so furious they'd be determined to get their revenge. So, yes, they would come after her all right, Ros guessed.

'Come on, boy, let's get a move on,' Ros, lying flat almost along Mantola's neck, murmured in his ear. 'Not too fast but a bit faster than this, Manty.'

From what she'd been able to observe in the poorly-lit barn Mantola had lost weight since last she'd seen him. That was predictable, really. If the thieves had been intending to steal Alexander's Star and had then discovered they'd got the wrong horse, it would be natural for them to pay minimal attention to it until they could turn it into money. As long as it looked healthy enough and moved freely then it would surely sell for a 'decent' price in the auction ring. In any case, whatever price it fetched it would practically all be profit (having stolen Phil Swift's box, the thieves hadn't even had to provide their own transport when committing the crime). So Mantola would probably have been given only the basic feeds he needed to keep him well enough to attract bids.

But he gave no sign of deprivation of any kind as he quickened in response to his rider's directions. She sensed he was just as delighted by their reunion as she was. Probably he realized they were now heading for home, even though this particular territory was unfamiliar to him. From a canter he moved up into a half-speed gallop. Mantola had never really been headstrong and now he picked his way around the possible pitfalls just like an old campaigner. Just once, on the edge of a soggy patch, he stumbled slightly and automatically slowed down.

That was when Ros heard the sounds of pursuit. Or, anyway, what she took to be pursuit. For, plainly enough on the still night air, she heard someone calling out; and then the whicker of a horse. Mantola's ears shot forward as he tried to detect the direction from which the sounds came. Ros, running her palm along his neck, now fast, now slow, could feel her heart beginning to thump, thump, thump in rising alarm. For the moment it wasn't fear; but she couldn't prevent herself from moistening her lips with an anxious tongue. Should she stop altogether or gallop as fast as possible away from the noises she'd heard?

Then, more distinctly this time, she heard a voice: 'Could've gone that way, leads towards the village. Reckon she'd be making for there.'

Ros was thankful it wasn't Tony Vasson's voice. But then, she hadn't imagined he would be the one to follow her because she doubted if he'd been involved in the kidnapping of Mantola. It was probably just a coincidence that he was attending the auction. In any case, for once he was in no position to seize any horse he fancied, as he did on the gallops. He might even have some difficulty in walking after what she'd done to his foot!

The reply, whatever it was, she couldn't make out: just a muted response of some sort. But, presumably, the second man was agreeing with the first for otherwise the conversation would have continued. And it didn't. At least, she could no longer hear any voices. Ros wished she could have seen which direction he was indicating. For all she knew the pursuers might even now be coming towards her. She was on the edge of high ground – the ridge was just over to their left – and it suddenly occurred to her that they might be visible as a silhouette on the skyline. Hastily she slid from Mantola's back to reduce their profile.

'Come on, Manty,' she said softly, still stroking his neck with one hand while taking his head collar with the other. 'We're going to hide ourselves over there, among the trees, until the coast's clear. So don't make any noise or we've had it.'

She'd brought a bag of boiled sweets but didn't dare offer one now because even the sound of his scrunching could carry. But Mantola had smelt or sensed their presence in her pocket and he began to nuzzle her in an effort to make her part with his prize.

'Later,' she whispered, 'later! Don't make a fuss, Manty.'

Twice before reaching the trees she paused to listen again: and to study the skyline. But there was neither sound nor sight of the men on horseback. And Mantola was no longer interested in distant sounds of other horses. He'd probably had enough of unwanted company in the past couple of weeks, Ros reasoned. All that interested him was the sweets in her pocket; and as soon as they were in the shelter of the copse she rewarded him with one. It disappeared with astonishing speed even for a horse which had always eaten up its feeds rapidly. Angela Sagaro approved of good 'doers' and in that respect Mantola came high up on her list.

Ros leaned against the trunk of a sapling. Suddenly, she felt tired out. The tension of the past few hours was taking its toll on her. She could have stretched out and fallen asleep in an instant. She shook herself vigorously; and then, to Mantola's obvious surprise, she began to run, quickly, on the spot. That, she knew, would wake her up. Sometimes she'd had to carry out that exercise early in the morning when she really felt like death after a late night but still had to go to the stables to do her work.

There'd been no sounds or movement of any kind to alarm them for perhaps half an hour and Ros judged that they should leave their hiding-place now. Their pursuers, she was confident, had moved away; if they were laying an ambush then all she could hope was that somehow she and Mantola would avoid it. In any case, the route she planned to take to Tildown House was circuitous. Mantola appeared quite fit and, as she'd discovered as soon as they paused in the copse, there was no heat in his off-fore. So perhaps the bandage he'd managed to discard in the Swift horsebox hadn't been necessary anyway!

The snapping of a twig underfoot almost as soon as they set off was the only alarming sound they heard. Ros hoisted herself on to Mantola's back and automatically he took that as a sign to quicken his pace. The area they were in was familiar to her because it adjoined the gallops, owned by a racing stable, at the top of the Downs. There were really no places at all for concealment up there. Moreover, in the slowly improving light she now had a good field of vision.

All the same, she felt enormously relieved when they reached the place where she'd left her bike and Mantola's saddle and tack. Her suppressed fear had been that someone would discover her things and wait murderously for her to collect them. Hurriedly she saddled up, remembering, surprisingly and pointlessly, really, the views of a girl she'd known at school who described riding horses bareback as 'just a circus trick, not to be tried by proper riders'.

Ros agreed with her. Even though riding without a saddle wasn't difficult with her experience, it wasn't something she enjoyed. Now, as she settled herself in the most comfortable position and turned Mantola's head towards home, she was thankful she'd planned with such care. How long her bike would have to be left under the hawthorn hedge she had no idea; but that hardly mattered now.

'Come on, Manty, the worst is over,' she told him. 'Soon you'll be rolling around in your own box and I'll be making you look all lovely again. And perhaps . . .'

But she didn't dare give voice yet to her greatest desire.

As his hooves began to ring out on the cobbled area at the

foot of Up-and-Down Lane her worries flooded back. If anyone was waiting for them, it would be somewhere around here. Her unease communicated itself to Mantola who began to play up, something he hadn't done on this spot for a very long time. To Ros, every deep shadow was menacing. Each one she passed was like a warning, telling her to be ready to run, run, run. She crouched in the saddle, wishing she'd alerted Lydia to what she was doing and asked her to meet them on their return. So much she had accomplished entirely on her own; and yet now she wanted the comfort of another voice, another, friendly, presence. and she was almost home. 'Really,' she told herself, 'that's a stupid way to go on! Stop thinking like that. You'll be there in a minute.'

So they were. All her fears about being ambushed had come to nothing. The horse-stealers, if that's who her pursuers were, had either lost their way or lost their nerve so close to the village itself. So, probably, they'd never have to pay for their crime. Now that Mantola was back, the police would probably lose interest in the case (not that they'd shown much in the first place, Ros reflected ruefully). Pity it wasn't like the old days when horse-stealing was a capital crime and thieves might be strung up by the neck when they were caught. Ros had read about that and thought how fitting the punishment was. Nothing would persuade her that retribution on that scale was a bit too drastic.

Mantola clattered into the yard with understandable eagerness as soon as Ros unlocked the gate. She could hear some of the other horses moving about in response to familiar sounds; but there was silence everywhere else. Then, to her great surprise, she saw a light go on in the house – and then another. Moments later she heard bolts being withdrawn from the door into the yard: and Angela Sagaro appeared, stave in hand. She looked utterly astonished.

'Rosalind! How on earth have you managed to find him? I can't believe it! D'you know, I thought you were an intruder, somebody trying to steal another of my horses.'

Ros grinned. 'Well, I suppose I have been stealing a horse in one way! I mean, it was the only way I could get Mantola back.'

Angela, who was wearing a thermal waistcoat and baggy trousers over pyjamas of a startling pink shade, was only half-listening. Instinctively she was checking the horse for any signs of heat in his off-fore before studying the rest of him.

'Well, he *seems* pretty well, though I'll have to give him a thorough examination in the morning,' she declared with evident relief in her voice. 'I'll get the vet in, of course. Have you *ridden* him back?'

'Had to. There was no other way of getting him here. You see – '

'But the saddle – and the tack – it's all mine! How on earth did you arrange that?'

'Well, it's a long story – '

'I'm sure it is, Rosalind. And I don't want to hear it now because you look all in. You've obviously had a – an exhausting time and no end of obstacles to overcome, I can imagine. You need a proper sleep, my dear.'

'Oh, I'll be all right, Mrs Sagaro. I mean, I've got to see to Mantola and – '

'That you haven't! That's my job. The least I can do after your heroic efforts. Your job is to get your head down and be fit enough to look after your horses tomorrow – or rather, later today!'

'But I want to tell you all that's happened. It's amazing how – '

'I'm sure it is, and I'm sure it must have been. But a good story will always keep, Rosalind. It may even get better because you've waited to tell it. And if I know Sir Alan Needwood he'll want to hear all the details, too – hear them

113

from you. First thing I'll be doing after breakfast is ringing him.'

Ros, who hadn't been able to prevent herself from reaching out for the dandy brush, let her hand drop. 'D'you think he'll come over, then, to hear what happened and see Mantola?'

'I'm sure of it. Just because he's not over here every five minutes, like some owners, to see whether we've ruined his precious horse doesn't mean that he doesn't care. I know for a fact that he does. And you know he approves of you, Rosalind.'

'But do you think he'll still let me ride Mantola in the Marathon? I mean, it's next week and – '

'It all depends if the horse is fit, doesn't it? That's the first priority. So – '

'Well, *of course*, I know Manty will have to be fit!' Rosalind was a little exasperated by Angela's punctiliousness. 'I mean, he may decide not to bother with the race this year and – '

'My dear, after what you've gone through to get his horse back for him, how can he possibly refuse you?'

'No,' said Ros emphatically, her confidence suddenly returning, 'he can't, really, can he?'

Postscript

'But what do you think your chances are?' Lydia asked for the umpteenth time as she stroked Mantola's nose.

'I've told you, Lyd, how on earth can I judge!' Ros replied, striving to remain calm. 'There's no form to go on, is there? This race is a one-off. So nobody really knows anything. You should have asked Agatha Elliott to look in her crystal ball. Then we'd all know the outcome.'

Lydia wasn't to be put off. 'But now you've seen the other runners you must have formed some idea of what you're up against.'

'All right, I'll give you a rundown,' Ros said positively, to please her friend. 'Manty is the most handsome horse so if looks count most he'll win easily. The favourite looks to be carrying far too much weight, below the saddle as well as above it; that's his real handicap. That grey, Go Now, is in too much of a lather, must be the nervous sort. Looks it, too. So he's probably sweated his chances away. I think that big chestnut, the one with the big white blaze, is the likeliest type. Strong – must be – and a good mover. Don't know about his rider, though. May be inexperienced.'

'That one's called As Yet,' Lydia supplied. 'Chap I met when you were saddling up told me he was backing that one and he thought he was on to a real winner. Of course, I told him Mantola is the one with real class. Know what he said, Ros?'

'Haven't a clue.'

'That he preferred *you* to the horse where looks are concerned!'

Ros laughed. It was nice to have a compliment like that; but she hoped it wasn't the only success she'd have today. Her heart was still set on winning the Midthorpe Marathon, the unique race that was more like a cross-country test than anything else.

The prize itself was really insignificant in monetary terms because it was a fixed sum that derived from the interest paid on a very ancient legacy; but the trophy, held for a year, was a cherished possession and the prestige of winning was high. The runner-up did best financially because he or she collected all the entry fees. There was nothing at all, except personal satisfaction, for finishing in third place. No previous winner was allowed to compete again but some horses had finished runner-up more than once. Tell It Again, second the previous year, was obviously one of the fancied horses this time but Hernando Cortez was the outright favourite. Ros didn't believe that any of them could defeat Mantola – just so long as Manty was fit enough for the race. And how fit he was no one could tell in advance.

During his ordeal in the hands of the kidnappers he'd lost weight, undoubtedly because of inadequate feeding but also probably through fretting. In the ten days since he'd been back at Tildown House his condition had improved considerably but, of course, he hadn't been subjected to any searching tests. He looked well: but, as everyone in racing knows, looks are often deceptive.

'I'd love you to win and I know the race means a lot to you, my dear,' Sir Alan told Ros before they set off for the course in the most luxurious horsebox she'd ever seen. 'But I know you won't give him too hard a race whatever happens.'

Ros interpreted that as a request, rather than a demand, to treat the horse as tenderly as possible and not to allow her natural ambition to cloud her judgement over what Mantola was capable of in a race over a distance that might be beyond him. Sir Alan really did have a lot of affection for the horse he'd so nearly lost and Ros was grateful the old man felt like that. Far too many owners seemed to be concerned only about the prestige and prize money their horses could earn for them. Really, she didn't need any reminder at all to take care of her mount at all times but she accepted that Sir Alan was entitled to pass such a comment.

The eight runners were now circling round at the start as their riders sought to calm their own nerves as well as their horses'. Ros knew only one of her rivals, Suzanne Almond-bury, a girl of about thirty, slim, efficient and very talented; she was on Tell It Again, a bay very much on his toes and apparently eager to make up for his narrow defeat the previous year. She and Suzanne had acknowledged each other's presence with a nod and a bleakish sort of smile; there was too much tension in the air to launch into any sort of conversation.

Lydia, who'd positioned herself by the starting line, was planning to cut through the wood that the runners would skirt so that she would have a chance of seeing the finish of the race at Tuckington crossroads where, traditionally, those who completed the course were treated to a dish of rum-and-plum pudding prepared by the landlord of the Lion and the Lamb, a landmark for centuries at the place where five roads converged. Ros, Lydia thought, looked as cool as anyone but Mantola was now sweating up a bit. She had her fingers crossed that his off-fore wasn't troubling him again.

The flag fell with some of the runners still well short of the starting line but, with more than four miles to be travelled, a leisurely start hardly seemed to matter. Hernando Cortez's beefy rider, however, urged his horse into a clear lead; the favourite had a marked dislike of being in close contact with other horses during a race and so he must either lead or fall in behind everyone else. His owner-rider preferred to dictate terms from the front. Ros ranged alongside Suzanne on Tell It Again, having decided that she was the one to keep company with over this tricky course; as last year's runner-up Suzanne would surely know how to pace herself and Ros was content to accept her lead for the time being.

The course, which Ros had walked a couple of times, initially followed what was always called the smugglers' route from the edge of the wood, down into a fold in the hillside and alongside a lazy stream before rising very sharply indeed to a natural saddle on Clover Hill. The descent to Tuckington could be perilous in places where spring water washed across the stony path and in the history of the Midthorpe several riders had come to grief when trying to overtake on that section. The next stretch was through the wood again and there the track was too narrow for any but the most precise passing manoeuvre. 'Whatever else, Ros, you've got to keep up with the pace,' she told herself. 'If you're not in the first three coming down the hill, you've had it. No one can win this race from the back.'

The grey, Go Now, suddenly cruised up on the inside and Ros glanced across at the rider. After her experience with Giselle Cornthwaite she was rather wary of females on greys but surely this one couldn't be so viciously treacherous as Giselle. In fact, the girl was concentrating so hard on keeping her mount settled that she seemed entirely unaware of Ros's interest. By now Hernando Cortez was at least six lengths clear of the field which, after the trio comprising Go Now, Tell It Again and Mantola, was well strung out. It was only in the wooded section that the course was marked with coloured tape and thus spectators were likely to encroach on to the track at almost any point; some determined camera enthusiasts even stepped out in front of the leading horse to take head-on shots, scurrying to safety in the nick of time. William Porter, the merchant banker riding his own gelding, Hernando Cortez, waved furiously at them to keep out of the way and threw out a few choice comments for good measure. The knots of passive spectators were quite good-humoured and prepared to applaud every horse that went by, whether it was carrying their bets or not.

Ros had decided that she should start to pick up on the leader as she followed the course of the stream. Mantola gave the impression that he was enjoying himself and that he would respond instantly to whatever she asked of him. A narrow, undulating track like this one wasn't really in his favour – his smooth, gliding action was much better suited to a galloping surface – but she was confident he would adapt to it. All that was needed now was just a quick word in his ear and he quickened immediately. Ros was immensely cheered by that response.

So the grey fell away behind her as Mantola closed on Tell It Again and the outright leader, Hernando Cortez. Suzanne Almondbury's sprightly bay accelerated, too, as Mantola caught him up and for several metres they moved as one, giving some watchers the impression that already there was a real battle in progress for second place. Ros wasn't displeased or worried about the proximity of Tell It Again; in fact, he was shielding Mantola from the stream and that was a distinct advantage in the light of Mantola's distaste for ponds and running water.

Then, as the stiff climb up to the saddle of Clover Hill came into sight, Mantola edged ahead of his nearest rival. Ros felt his muscles begin to tighten as he wound himself up for real action: and it was an exhilarating experience. He was used to working on the uphill gallops at the top of Up-and-Down Lane and he didn't need encouragement to tackle the slope with zest. Hernando Cortez was still some four lengths in the lead but Ros suspected that the surplus weight he was carrying would become an anchor on a gradient of this severity. She risked a glance over her shoulder ('Never, ever, look back during a race unless it's a life-or-death situation,' the first trainer she'd ridden for had always advised) and saw that Tell It Again was only a couple of lengths behind them while the rest were now thoroughly strung out. However, one runner that had made useful progress was As Yet, his white blaze clearly evident at Go Now's shoulder.

The favourite wasn't coming back to her after all. In spite of his size, William Porter was an accomplished and astute rider, not at all the burden to his partner that he might appear to be. As they approached the summit he even managed to give Hernando Cortez a breather. Porter's belief that he could lead all the way was undiminished. He really didn't care at all about who was on his heels. So far he hadn't had to ask his mount to exert himself in any way.

The instinct was always to pause at the summit, though not just to admire the view. The descent of Clover Hill was a distinctly tricky proposition for the path was strewn with flints and even quite large stones, and the edges often crumbled. Many contestants in previous Marathons had surveyed the route ahead of them with dismay bordering on horror, and gone on to suffer the consequences of their fear. William Porter didn't pause at all but sailed serenely over the crest as though taking no notice whatsoever of the new hazards ahead. Ros knew that Mantola wouldn't enjoy the descent half as much as the climb; but she mustn't let him know that she knew that. As long as he had confidence in her as pilot, all would be well, she believed.

It was the whooping cheers of a group of spectators, coupled with a stone kicked up by a sliding hoof, that caused the first disaster of the race. The victim was Go Now. He was one of the horses that didn't care at all for the sharpness of the gradient and, in an effort to pull himself up, he began to slither; at precisely that moment Tell It Again, too, was unsure of his footing and kicked up a stone that flew into Go Now's chest like a bullet. The small crowd gathered just below the summit set up an excited cry as they saw what was happening to Tell It Again and that unnerved

Go Now completely. Trying to jump his way out of trouble by getting clear of the track he plunged helplessly into the hillside.

Luckily for Go Now's rider, she was flung clear before the horse lost his footing completely and took a crashing fall; and then, sensibly, he lay there until he recovered his breath. A spectator was able to grab hold of the reins and make sure he didn't bolt when he was on his feet again.

Tell It Again had made one mistake, but it was only one. He was familiar with this circuit and Suzanne had no fears about the fierceness of the slope. Just when Ros had thought it almost impossible to pass, Suzanne overtook her to move into second place. She had her sights on taking control before they reached the final wooded section that ended at Tuckington crossroads. It was because she'd delayed the challenge that she'd failed to win the race the previous year.

Ros, not enjoying the downhill section any more than Mantola was, felt alarmed: and, moments later, she felt still worse when the big, white-faced chestnut As Yet came clattering by. His jockey had decided before the race began that the best tactic would be to follow Suzanne Almondbury, the most experienced rider on this circuit. He, too, realized that it could be fatal to his chances of success to wait too long before seizing the lead. His horse was an out-and-out stayer and therefore would be much better suited to running the race from the front. As Yet, not troubled at all by the treacherous terrain, moved easily into second place to resounding cheers from his supporters, some of whom really could recognize a dark horse when they saw one, whatever his colour! For once the bookies had been generous when they priced him, unaware of his versatility over a variety of circuits in his native New Zealand. Meanwhile, one of the back markers stumbled awkwardly after trying to jump a stream running across the path and his rider, fearing the worst, pulled him up, reducing the field to six.

121

'Come on, Manty, come on, we can do better than this,' Ros urged.

Mantola was doing his best but gaining no ground on any of the three horses ahead of him. As the leader reached the bottom of the hill and entered the short stretch on the level to the edge of the wood, it was plain that his advantage was much reduced: As Yet had cut the gap to no more than a couple of lengths with Tell It Again right on his heels. William Porter used his whip to remind Hernando Cortez that the race wasn't over yet. The favourite, who'd been quite happy until that moment, started to sulk; what's more, he was aware that other horses were close to his tail. For Hernando the race was really over in spite of all William Porter's driving over the next hundred metres.

Lengthening his stride like the good horse he was, As Yet cruised into the lead. Ros gulped and asked Mantola for a bigger effort in the same moment that Suzanne started to ride in earnest. Now the crowd's enthusiasm began to reverberate all along the narrow track between the trees. Among them was Lydia. The moment she caught sight of Ros she began to wave both arms with enormous vigour, her injured humerus quite healed by now.

'Go ON, Ros, you can still do it!' she yelled. 'Don't give up!'

Ros heard her. She had no intention of giving up but was grateful for Lydia's support. Now, though, she sensed that the race was out of her grasp. She wished she'd ridden the course in advance (as she was entitled to do because only a small part of it was over private land) instead of just walking it. Then she would have been better prepared for that formidable downhill section; she would have gone into the lead before the summit so that Mantola could have been given a breather before being asked for his final effort.

She and Suzanne were neck-and-neck when they overtook the retreating Hernando Cortez and both realized they had no hope of catching the unstoppable As Yet. The race was now for second place, not for the prestige but for the prize-money. Just once, as they stormed past the last tree with Tuckington crossroads now in sight, Ros thought Mantola was faltering; but he was simply changing legs because of tiredness. His ordeal in the hands of the kidnappers had taken a lot out of him and he wasn't fully recovered. But his courage, and his undoubted class, kept him going, gun-barrel straight, to the finishing line.

Ros rode him just with hands and heels. No whip could make him give any more. And no more than ten metres from the post he got his head in front and kept it there.

'Great race, that,' Suzanne panted as they slowed their horses and shook hands. 'Pity neither of us actually won! Still, you know, there's next year. I don't believe in giving up.'

'Nor do I,' grinned Ros.